T

TH

TO GATHER THE WIND

BODIE & BROCK THOENE

THOMAS NELSON PUBLISHERS
Nashville

Published in Association with the literary agency of:

Alive Communications, Inc.
P.O. Box 49068
Colorado Springs, CO 80949

Published in Nashville, Tennessee, by Thomas Nelson, Inc.

Library of Congress Cataloging-in-Publication Data

Thoene, Brock, 1952—
　To gather the wind : a novel / Brock and Bodie Thoene.
　　　p.　cm.
　　ISBN 0-7852-8073-1 (pb)
　　I. Title
PS3570.H463L57　1997
813'.54—dc21　　　　　　　　　　　　　　　　　　97-5032
　　　　　　　　　　　　　　　　　　　　　　　　CIP

Printed in the United States of America

1 2 3 4 5 6 7　RRD　04 03 02 01 00 99 98

Other Books by
Bodie and Brock Thoene

CHAPTER 1

Nick Bledsoe, driver of the swaying Concord coach, plied the double fistful of ribbons in smooth succession to ease the six-up team around a bend. The stage road between the summit of the Sierra Nevada and the mining town of Placerville, California, followed the south fork of the American River. "Followed" was, in this case, a term loosely applied. Just below where Tamarack Creek joined the American, the river plunged some six hundred feet over a series of cascades into a granite chasm.

The trail adopted by the Pioneer Stage Company was not so exuberant. It prudently remained high on the hillside among the lofty sugar pines and incense cedars until gradually winding downward to rejoin the river at the way station known as Strawberry.

Bledsoe told me back in Genoa that he had traversed this stretch of road hundreds of times, through snow and rain even, and so the starlit and warm September night held no particular terrors. Still, the driver had a healthy respect for the narrow path. He kept plenty of distance between the rig and the right-hand edge of the roadway, since that side lay above the drop-off. It was not possible to hug the uphill rim too closely, because the stage road ran atop a ten-high embankment. A fine touch was required to keep the rig where it belonged. The concentration made Bledsoe bite his lower lip and kept him even quieter than his usual taciturn self.

The driver's lack of responsiveness made absolutely no difference to the man seated to his left on the box. Oliver Adonijah Turnipseed, known to all as Ollie, was the shotgun messenger employed by Wells, Fargo and Company. His job was to escort shipments of bullion from the mines east of the divide to Sacramento, California. Ollie's chatter was ceaseless, as if he thought it part of his sworn duty to see that no driver ever fell asleep. "Bit of south wind in the treetops," he observed. "Blow up a thunderstorm by tomorrow afternoon, don't you think, Nick?" It never bothered Ollie to receive only a grunt in reply. "Yep, be some lightning fires by tomorrow night. Been a right dry year, so far, ain't it? Still, the river ain't let up much. Listen to it roar. Man, I'd hate to go over the edge along here, wouldn't you? Smash this wagon to matchsticks and float 'em clean down to Sac City, eh Nick?"

Unperturbed by this cheerful thought, probably because Ollie made the same remark every trip, Bledsoe straightened his shoulders to relieve the strain from the lines and nudged the leaders into a tighter curve.

The top of the coach was without passengers that evening in 1857, though Bledsoe had known times when it was crammed. As many as seven full-grown men had jostled for place and held on for dear life on the traverse of the mountains. Stage travel was still the only way to get to the gold country settlements, and all manner of folks rode the coaches.

The three people sitting with me in the darkness inside the conveyance amply illustrated the point. Two of them, the portly Banker Frick and his equally rotund wife, were travelling from Genoa in the Carson Valley to his company's headquarters in San Francisco. Since business called for a stop at Placerville, the Fricks would keep to the stage as far as Sacramento, then go by steamboat downriver to Frisco.

The third occupant of the rig had come from much farther away. Eliza Richardson had been four days on the Overland stage from the Midwest to where she had boarded the Pioneer line coach. Her sensible slate-gray overdress looked little the worse for wear despite the alkali dust of the Carson Valley. Her hair was demurely tucked up inside a poke bonnet that matched her travel costume. The somber garb proclaimed proper modesty for an unaccompanied female, but Eliza's darting hazel eyes and the remembrance of freckles across her cheekbones suggested a lively spirit.

Frick and I had gallantly allowed the ladies to ride facing forward, so as to minimize the motion sickness induced by the rolling movement of the coach. This meant that my lanky, long-nosed, twenty-six-year-old frame sat directly across from Miss Richardson.

I had been aboard the same coach with her ever since Missouri, having begun my travels all the way back in New Jersey. My black dress suit showed creases where none were intended and somewhere between Omaha and Fort Kearny my fashionable bowler hat was crushed. I tried several times to engage Eliza in conversation, but general gawkiness seemed to come all over me like a rash when in the company of females. I surveyed my stained and worn clothing, saw again the hint of laughter on Eliza's face, and refrained from speaking. Over the whirring of the wheels, I could hear the conversation between the guard and the driver.

Nick Bledsoe clucked to the leaders, flicked the reins, and the bay horses leaned into the harness. The road had a brief uphill spell, climbing a hogback ridge before resuming its descent. Looming up out of the canyon was the gigantic granite monolith known locally as Lover's Leap. It towered at three times the height of the hundred-foot-tall pines and tapered to a jagged point at its top. The reinsman looked at the landmark blocking the lower half of the Big Dipper and sighed heavily. The despondent groan was not because he was exhausted or sad, but because Bledsoe felt the need to steel himself for what he knew Ollie was about to say.

"Can't see it myself," Ollie muttered right on cue, pointing at the saw-toothed crag. "Just 'cause Horace Greeley printed some folderol about Injun maidens and doomed lovers . . . bosh! Shoulda called it Sharktooth Rock or Spearpoint Cliff . . . somethin' that said what it looked like. Why, shoot fire, old Dat-so-naga said there weren't a lick of truth to that yarn a'tall. Injuns called it Eagle Rock, when they bothered to call it anything. Can you imagine that? Editor Horace high-an'-mighty Greeley printin' somethin' made up, just so's to fill up space in his newspaper. Kinda like flappin' your gums just to hear yourself talk, ain't it?"

The reinsman disregarded even this unintended humor. Tucking his wiry black beard down lower into his shirt collar, Bledsoe ignored Ollie. Fifteen minutes to Strawberry and a cup of coffee. Then an hour's run to Silver Fork, where the relief driver would take over and Bledsoe could turn in till picking up the outbound run tomorrow morning.

The first hint Bledsoe had that something was wrong was a snort given by the near leader. The bay horse made a sharp cough, as mountain-bred horses do when they scent a bear or a cougar. Then, just at the peak of the rise in the middle of another sharp bend, the leaders reared abruptly and the swing team and wheelers jolted to a prancing stop. A tree had fallen across the road, blocking it completely.

Mrs. Frick gave a brief chorus of feminine shrieks. Bledsoe swore angrily and fought the team to a standstill. Setting the brake lever, he wrapped the ribbons around the handle. Ollie, jolted from his monologue, nervously reached for the coach gun beneath the seat.

At the moment that his fingers touched the checkered stock of the sawed-off double-barrel, a rasping voice erupted from the shadows at the side of the road. "Guard!" it ordered. "Easy with that scattergun! Toss it over!" Then the commanding tone continued, "You, Driver, keep your hands where I can see 'em! You inside the coach! This is a holdup! Don't try anything stupid and you won't get hurt!"

Ollie complied, slowly lifting the Lovell twelve gauge by three fingers around the barrels. He dropped the weapon in the soft dirt. At the quiet thump seven figures materialized from the manzanita scrub around the stage.

All the attackers were dressed in oilcloth dusters that covered them from ankle to neck. Every man wore a hat pulled low across his forehead and each face was swathed in a dark bandana. Each bandit held a six-gun at the ready.

Their leader spoke again. "Throw down the pouches!"

Ollie glanced at Nick Bledsoe, then fumbled in the leather boot under his seat and produced a single canvas sack, which he tossed to the ground.

"All of them!" the bandit chief snarled, waving his pistol.

The Wells, Fargo guard complied, throwing two more bags of gold bullion beside the first. "Now the strongbox!" the robber ordered.

"Ain't got one," Ollie replied.

"Throw down the box or I'll shoot you off there and get it myself!" The double-locked iron box bounced to the ground. Two of the highwaymen dragged it to the side of the road and smashed it open while three others retrieved the sacks of gold bars. On the uphill side of the trail other horses could be heard nervously puffing and snorting as the bandits transferred the loot.

"You won't get by with this," Ollie countered. "Wells, Fargo don't take kindly to them as makes free with their shipments. No sir! You'll be hunted like the low varmints you are. Sheriff will get up a posse . . ."

"Give it a rest," the leader of the thieves directed, putting the barrel of the thirty-six caliber pistol alongside Ollie's knee. "'Less you want me to plug your yap for you." Ollie subsided at once. "You in the coach. Step out here!" The two women, Frick, and I emerged from the rig and lined up beside the wagon. "Empty your pockets and handbags!"

Superintendent Frick looked sullen; his wife, terrified. Mrs. Frick fumbled and fluttered her way through her beaded handbag, dribbling coins, mirror, and comb onto the ground before the bandit chief grabbed it from her and emptied it in a heap. From the debris he selected a bracelet and a wad of cash.

"That bullion must weigh a lot," Eliza observed coolly. "It will slow down your escape."

I felt my eyes widen at the girl's audacity. Making hushing sounds, I murmured, "These men should not be trifled with."

But the robber captain did not seem annoyed. "Thank you for your concern," he growled. Then clearing his throat, he added, "I have plenty of help." From the banker he took a gold watch and a fat wallet; from me he got a pocket watch that had been my father's and a single five dollar gold piece. "Slim pickings," he growled. "What about you, young lady?"

Eliza kicked a small satchel toward the man. "See for yourself," she said. "No jewelry, no money. Oh, I do have two postage stamps . . . would you like them?"

The bandit chuckled. "How about that, boys?" he called to his accomplices. "Should we take up a collection to give to these poor folks?" There was a chorus of rough laughter. "Drag the tree out of the way," he concluded roughly. "Be quick." In a moment the way forward was clear once more. "Get back aboard," he said.

Wheeling abruptly on his heel, Banker Frick stepped into the coach. When Mrs. Frick turned to hoist herself up to the stage, starlight glinted on something at her throat; something previously unseen. "Hold it," the highwayman ordered. He reached out and grabbed the necklace concealed by the high collar.

Maizie Frick let out a scream that startled the horses, making them lunge forward and pitching her down to the ground. The bandit captain, unbalanced by the sudden shift and still grasping the jewelry, stumbled as well.

It looked to me like the highwayman was throwing Mrs. Frick to the ground. "Let go of her!" I shouted, grabbing the bandit by the shoulder and pulling him away.

With a backhand swing, the highwayman whipped his pistol barrel against my skull, just above the right ear. I staggered sideways, going down on one knee. The robber wrenched the necklace until it broke, then turned and coolly kicked me in the ribs. My breath went out in a choking cough.

He was drawing back his heavy boot for another deliberate blow to my side when Eliza threw herself between me and my attacker. "Enough!" she shouted. "Mister Ryland was defending *her* . . . something you would not know anything about. Leave him alone!"

I had not even thought she knew my name.

"Come on," one of the accomplices urged. "We been too long already."

The robber chief agreed, gruffly ordering the women into the coach and throwing me in after. "Get going," he ordered Bledsoe.

The stagecoach jerked forward down the trail, rounding a curve to the right. At that moment Frick slid a hideout gun from his sleeve, leaned out the window of the rig, and fired a single round. The twenty-two caliber shell popped feebly and the bullet went wide, sparking against a rock.

The bandit captain's Colt flipped up in his hand and he triggered a return shot just as the coach disappeared around the bend. The slug took Nick Bledsoe below his right arm, smashing two ribs and puncturing his lung.

"Nick!" Ollie sputtered. "Are you hit? Is it bad? Can you make it to Strawberry? Do you want me to take the reins? Shall I . . ."

The stage clattered down the trail toward the American River, with Bledsoe leaning heavily against Ollie. The driver pressed his elbow tight against the wound and gritted his teeth with pain. "You'll have to help me," he said to the guard. "And by all that's holy, don't yammer or I'll throw you off!"

Of course I was told the last of this later, since at the time I was lying, barely conscious, on the floor inside the coach.

The stage stop called Strawberry was at the base of granite cliffs in the bottom of the gorge. Just below where the American River made a sweeping turn to the south, the stream slowed enough to deposit acres of clay and create a high mountain meadow. Well watered and grassy, it was a natural pasture. Ever since the emigrant days of the forties, travellers across the Sierra had stopped there to rest and feed their stock.

Charlie Watson, the proprietor of the way station, had been a driver on the Pioneer line. That was before he discovered that it was more lucrative and less dangerous to sell meals to passengers than to transport them. In the short summers he cut the grass in his pasture and sold bundles of hay for as high as two dollars apiece.

The night of the holdup, Watson was forking hay into the loft of the cavernous barn when he heard the stage approaching. He squinted at the stars thoughtfully and frowned. The stage was late. That was not like Bledsoe. Nick never waited for anyone, be they bank president or newspaper editor, and if delayed for any reason always made up the time somewhere on the way.

Pitchfork still in his hands, Watson stood in the lighted doorway of the station when the coach rolled up. "Nick," he yelled before he got a clear view of the box. "What ails you? You're late."

"Jumping Jehoshaphat!" the gabbling voice of Ollie Turnipseed retorted. "Are you gonna stand around jawin' all night, Charlie? Cain't you see we got trouble? Nick's been shot! Give me a hand here, will you?"

With the last reserve of his strength, Nick Bledsoe clapped his boot on the brake lever. He passed the reins to Ollie with a groan and collapsed over the seat. Bent at the waist and leaning forward, Bledsoe would have fallen off the coach if Watson had not thrown aside the pitchfork and run up to catch him.

Charlie Watson tried to ask what had happened, but Ollie's explanation ran over the top of the question. "Holdup!" Ollie declared. "A dozen masked men jumped us behind Lover's Leap. They took the bullion and the box; robbed the passengers, too. Shot poor Nick here."

"Help me get him inside," Watson ordered, catching Bledsoe across his shoulders.

The driver was unconscious. His shirt was sticky with blood from neck to waistband and soaked clear through.

The coach door opened and Mr. Frick emerged. "Help my wife," he demanded. "Give me a hand with her."

Frick was roughly shoved aside from behind by an indignant Eliza. "She's not hurt! Just had a fainting spell. But there is another injured man here."

"Was this a holdup or a massacre?" Watson wondered aloud. "Grant!" he shouted to the young stablehand inside the station. "Come here on the double!"

As Grant swept a pile of pots, pans, and dishes off the trestle table, Watson laid Bledsoe down under the light of a coal oil lantern. When he saw the saturated crimson mass of the shirt and the ashen complexion of the driver's face, he whistled softly. Watson felt the driver's neck for a pulse, then laid his hand over Nick's heart.

Through the door came Grant and Ollie. They supported me between them, though I knew none of it at the time. I was semiconscious, but my legs refused to obey me and I wobbled as if drunk. Eliza bustled in after, directing Ollie to deposit me on the floor near the woodstove.

"Just what is the meaning of this treatment?" a red-faced Banker Frick demanded as he half carried and half dragged Mrs. Frick into the station. "First a holdup and then this complete and utter disregard of my wife's well-being. The directors of the bank shall lodge . . ."

"Shut up," Watson said, shaking his fist under Frick's nose. Then dismissing the man as of no further consequence, Watson turned to Ollie and said, "He's dead, Ollie. Nick is dead."

There was a moment of stunned silence, then Eliza asked for a basin of water and a cloth to tend to my head wound. She knelt beside me and sponged the matted blood from my hair.

"Whillikers!" Ollie sputtered. "Nick dead? But he drove the coach down off the mountain! Never missed a curve, I tell you. He's a hero, Charlie, a hero. He brought us down safe even though he was dyin'!"

"How did this happen?" Watson said slowly. "What caused the gunplay?"

Looking up from tending me, Eliza said tartly, "It was he." She brandished the bloodstained cloth like an accusing finger toward Frick. "After the robbery was all done and no one hurt, *he* pulled out a pistol and fired for no reason. That's when the driver got shot."

"It's not true," Frick blustered. "The young woman is confused. The bandits meant to kill us all; leave no witnesses. I was defending us."

"Ask Ollie," Eliza suggested. "How many shots were fired and when?"

Ollie substantiated Eliza's recollection.

"What do you say to that?" Watson inquired.

"It was her back talk that got the robbers riled up," Frick said, throwing the blame on Eliza. "She raved and carried on and argued like a crazy woman. Could have got us all killed!"

Then everyone was talking at once. Ollie chattered about what a hero Nick was. Eliza, flushed with anger, rebuked Frick, who responded hotly that she had better watch her impertinent mouth. Frick's wife fanned herself frantically and swooned again.

"Hold it!" Charlie Watson roared. "There's been a killing. I'll drive the coach myself on down to Placerville; alert the sheriff. Those that are able can come along; the rest can stay here with Grant. Ollie, you'll have to come make your report for Wells, Fargo. They'll want to send an agent to take part in the investigation."

I startled everyone by speaking from where I was slumped on the floor. "Jack Ryland," I said, as if introducing myself to the room. "I need to make my report, too." My thoughts bubbled out of my mouth without the formality of organization. "I am an attorney."

"So?" Watson inquired. "Son, I don't think you're thinking straight. What's all this to you except a knock upside the ear?"

I shook my head slowly and grimaced as even that slight motion hurt terribly. "I'm an attorney for Wells, Fargo," I said. "In charge of robbery investigations."

CHAPTER 2

By the time Charlie Watson had whipped up the team and headed for Placerville and the sheriff, I was loaded into the back of a buckboard. No more animated than a side of bacon, I could neither applaud not protest. I found out later that Eliza Richardson recruited the stablehand to drive the rig to her father's home farther down the south fork of the American.

Watson stirred the countryside to a flurry. He turned out Deputy Sheriff Jim Hume and Hume straightaway called up a posse. Bledsoe had been a popular man. Stage drivers were looked upon as a special breed at all times, and Ollie's expansive report of Bledsoe's heroics guaranteed a huge outcry for swift action. By the time pale dawn was breaking over the Sierra, Hume had collected fifty men from all the settlements in the area.

Banker Frick tried to polish his tarnished reputation by self-importantly furnishing descriptions of the robbers. The problem was, other than a head count, what could he say except that they all wore slickers and masks?

It was Eliza whose quick wit again furnished the only real clue. She told Watson that the reason she kept provoking the bandit chief to conversation was so as to hear as much of his voice as possible. She described it as the voice of a young man, but roughened by whiskey or tobacco; below medium pitch and bearing down on words ending in "r." This information Watson dutifully reported to Deputy Hume.

Hume dispatched riders in groups of six to scour the canyons and settlements east and west and south of the robbery site. He himself led a double contingent north over the hills toward Georgetown. At each mining camp along Mosquito Creek, Texas Canyon, and up Rock Creek, the posse quizzed the miners about anyone passing through during the night and about any strangers in the area.

The search proved futile until they reached Cincinnati Flat, midway between Gopher Hill and Griswold's. An old-timer named Slate, standing knee-deep in a prospecting hole, allowed that someone had interrupted his sleep to ask about a missing horse. The stranger said he had been thrown while riding across the hillside. He thought the horse might have wandered toward the campfires. "Gave him a piece of my mind, I did," Slate stated forcefully. "Asked him if he saw any sucha horse thereabouts. Couldn't he see for hisself there weren't no horse critter there? What'd he come botherin' sleepin' folks for?"

Hume suppressed a grin and asked if Slate could describe the nighttime caller. "Can't say so," Slate announced. "It bein' on the dark side o' dawn a'course. The hombre had his hat pulled down and was done up in a duster; though it were a pretty warm night at that."

Thanking the miner, Hume turned to his group. "Tim Flynn," he said to his second in command. "This is our first break. If he hasn't stolen another horse somewhere, we'll take him pretty easy. You and your five follow Dutch Creek. My bunch will stay east of Mount Murphy, and we'll meet up again at Sailor Flat. Got it?"

The terrain on the west slope of Mount Murphy was steep and cluttered with scrub oak and buckeye. The buckeye trees were in blossom, each branch holding aloft a stock of flowers like a pale flame. The heads of the horses drooped as the sun passed midday and the breeze died.

Flynn called a halt by the side of a heap of rubble that had onetime been a rock fort. An Irishman named Murphy, with a deathly fear of Indians, built the redoubt for protection against an attack that never came. He even bought an antique Russian cannon off of Captain Sutter, but the ancient weapon was never fired in anger. Eventually both Murphy and the cannon had moved away, leaving only the mound and the name to mark the spot.

The men stepped from their mounts into a shady patch. Their clothes stuck to their bodies and sweat dripped into their eyes. The eagerness of a pursuit begun at daybreak had been replaced by a sullen spirit.

Flynn passed around a knapsack of hard biscuits. Two of the posse members crumbled the crackers into tin cups of water and ate. The others ignored the dry bread altogether and opted for long pulls on their canteens.

The divide between the middle and south forks of the American River is called the "listening hills." Some quirk of the air and the landscape makes it possible to hear a dog bark from a mile away; a gunshot two miles or more.

Up the slope toward the circle of weary riders came the sound of someone calling an animal. "Here, boy," the voice coaxed. "Come here, now. Come here and get this grain."

Flynn shushed the conversation of the posse and raised himself to peer over the rim of a boulder. At first he could not see where the words came from, but then in a clearing about half a mile away, a lineback buckskin stumbled into view. The horse was dragging a broken rein. About every third step it would place a hoof on the trailing lead and jerk itself to a halt. Midway in the clearing it looked over its shoulder back the way it had come.

"Come here, cuss you," said a medium-height, narrow-shouldered man who emerged from a clump of chaparral behind the buckskin. "Hold still, will you?"

"Saddle up, boys," Flynn said softly. "I think we've got our man."

The solitary figure was so intent on catching the wayward mount that he did not notice the approach of the armed riders until they had him surrounded. He had finally gotten near enough to the skittish horse to pounce on the dragging rein when Tim Flynn spurred out of the brush with his Colt Navy drawn and cocked. "Stand still and get your hands up!" he ordered. "Come on in, men."

"What is this?" the lone fellow asked, looking nervously at the armed men emerging all around him. "If this is a holdup, you're out of luck, friends. I haven't got a cent . . . I'm flat busted. Got nothing but a sack of parched corn."

"That's rich," Flynn said with a smirk. "Play it off like we're the robbers. What's in those saddlebags then?" Flynn gestured with the muzzle of the revolver toward a pair of bulging packs tied behind the buckskin's saddle.

"Search me," the captured man said. "Look, my name's Baker. Tom Baker. I just walked in from Yuba City. I got no money and I lost my mule in a card game back in Downieville. Then, about ten this morning, I spotted this gelding and I've been trying to catch him ever since. What's all this about, anyhow?"

"It's about robbery and murder and it's gonna be about hangin'," Flynn said. "Ain't that right?" There was a growl of agreement from the posse.

"I ain't done nothing," Baker protested. "I told you this ain't my horse . . . I wasn't trying to steal him or nothing . . . just use him to ride into town."

"Hold him," Flynn commanded. Two of the posse members flanked Baker.

"I said I ain't done nothing," Baker repeated. "And I don't take kindly to being manhandled." Snickers ran through the posse. Outnumbered six to one at about a hundred and forty pounds, Baker looked no threat to back his words with his fists.

"Go on," Flynn ordered his troop.

Waiting until the two posse members were in the line of Flynn's fire, Baker allowed them to grasp his arms and then by suddenly throwing himself backward, swung them hard into each other, tangling them in legs and fists. Slapping the buckskin on its rump, Baker ran alongside the startled animal, then jumped aboard at a gallop.

The boom of Flynn's Colt echoed and a bullet whizzed past Baker's head. "Don't kill him, Tim," one of the others protested. "What if he's innocent?"

The lineback sprinted across the clearing, but before he could break free, two of the posse cut him off. Baker jerked the gelding to a sliding stop and cut off at right angles to his first path.

Despite the objection, Flynn fired again, the slug shattering on a heap of rocks right in front of Baker's line of travel. Once again Baker yanked the buckskin to the side. He set the gelding at a pile of brush, intending to jump the chaparral and escape the trap.

The light tan horse shied at the last moment and Baker's left foot pulled free of the stirrup. He pitched heavily onto the ground, bounced up holding his elbow, and attempted to run again.

Flynn rode up behind him, twirling a loop.

Just as Baker scaled the trunk of a fallen oak, Flynn's lasso settled around his neck, jerking the fugitive to the ground. When Flynn backed his mount, the noose tightened about the captive's neck, cutting off his wind and dragging him roughly over brush and rocks. "Catch that horse!" Flynn ordered, smugly proud of his success. "Now we'll see!"

His hands tied behind his back and the loop of lariat still cinching his throat, Baker could only watch as the buckskin's saddlebags were dumped in the clearing. "Mighty heavy," one of the posse reported.

Upended in the blazing afternoon sun, a half dozen gold bars flashed with painful accusation. Each bore the inscribed stamp of Wells, Fargo and Company. "Dead broke, eh?" Flynn sneered. "Caught red-handed, I'd say."

"What are we gonna do with him?" one of Flynn's troopers inquired.

"Do?" Flynn replied, squinting into the pale, blue afternoon sky. "Here's the proof of his guilt, right? And he already tried to escape once, right? Let's hang him here and be done with it. We can take him back easier dead than alive."

"Shouldn't he get a chance to speak?" someone asked.

"I'll give him a chance," Flynn said grudgingly. "You got anything to say for yourself before we hang you for the murder of Nick Bledsoe?"

Baker tried to speak, but only a croak came out. He pointed to the loop around his neck and shook his head.

"He don't even deny it anymore, see? Enough messing around." Flynn walked his horse to an overhanging oak limb and tossed the free end of the lariat over the branch, then tied it to his saddle horn.

"Hold it!" Jim Hume demanded, trotting his horse into the clearing. "Heard the shooting clear around the hill and came on the run," he said. If the listening hills had brought about Baker's apprehension, the curious play of the echoes also intervened to postpone his execution. Hume looked down at the prisoner and at the heap of gold bullion. "You did good with the capture, Tim," he said to Flynn. "But this is not the bad old days in Hangtown. We have law and order here now, and fair trials."

"Yeah?" Flynn argued. "What kind of fair trial did Nick get, huh? What about his wife and kids?"

Casually laying the barrel of a twelve-gauge shotgun across the pommel of his saddle, Hume remarked, "I imagine that the Coloma jail is the closest hoosegow. Much obliged to you, Tim. I'll see to the prisoner."

I woke with a splitting headache that began at the entire right side of my head and tapered to a sharp point somewhere in the middle. It felt as if someone had been trying to make stove wood out of my skull and came near succeeding. The pain was accompanied by a dull roaring.

The next thing I noticed was that while I could hear a mosquito's whine and the soft chirping of crickets on my left side, I could make out nothing from the right. I was not certain if the blow had left me deaf in that ear, or if the dead silence might be due to the yards of bandage and padding in which my noggin was swaddled.

Raising my hand from where it lay folded across my chest, I moved to check the situation. This was a mistake. The roaring in my brainpan increased in volume until it was a ripsaw in full swing. I let my hand drop back; finding out if I still had an ear on that side could wait.

I elected to postpone opening my eyes as well, satisfying myself with trying to recollect where I was and how I had come to be there. I remembered the holdup, right up until the moment I got hit. Thereafter I only had bits and pieces. I recollected a gunshot and being slumped on the floor near a stove. I recalled that every time I awoke, another jolt of a wagon wheel over a tree root would pack me off again.

There was a girl. I could not remember her name, but she seemed to have something to do with my bandages and the cot on which I was lying.

It was the best I could do for the time. With the sweet smells of a mountain breeze fanning my eyelids, I allowed myself the luxury of falling back to sleep.

When next I woke I could feel a thread of the summer sun stitching a seam of warmth across my cheek. The pounding had subsided. This and a growl from my stomach convinced me that living might be tolerable, so I cautiously opened one eye.

I was in a high-ceilinged room of white painted sawn lumber. The sunlight was coming in through a window with a green sash. Outside the frame was the trunk of an oak. Without moving (something I was still reluctant to do) I could make out a dresser on the far wall, topped with a pitcher of water and a vase of purple wildflowers. Through the open window I could hear voices coming nearer the house, and I concentrated on making out the words.

It scared me to death! I could not understand anything being spoken. The speech all ran together in a kind of singsong melody. The consonants pattered like a fall of cutlery; the vowels brayed like Balaam's ass.

Sitting bolt upright, I slapped my bare feet on the plank floor. The noise of my awakening roused someone in an adjoining room. I heard chair legs scraping and footsteps coming hurriedly toward the bedroom door.

Halfway to my feet I tottered sideways. The door burst open and a short, bespectacled man with an unruly tangle of white hair and a stubble of white whiskers caught me and lowered me to a seat. Despite the early hour, a whiff of rye whiskey accompanied him into the room. "Easy, there, Mister Ryland!" he cautioned. "I do not allow patients to undo all my hard work by their recklessness! Where would my reputation be then?"

It was easy for me to agree. I nodded weakly and accepted a glass of water. Then it dawned on me that I understood his speech. There was no slurring. "Your voice . . ." I said, then stopped. Had I been hallucinating?

"My voice?" my doctor said quizzically. He regarded me over the top of his thick, round lenses and suggested that I might wish to lie back down.

"No," I protested. "I'm feeling better now. But I must thank you. You are Doctor . . . ?"

"Richardson," he offered. "Eliza brought you here in the middle of the night, screaming like a banshee that you had to be seen to at once. Sat up with you all night as well."

"Miss Richardson is your daughter, then?" This observation showed me to be dull as a post, but the good doctor did not mock me.

He nodded. "Said you are a hero. Made me tend to your wounds and this, mind, was my greeting after not seeing her for these three years past." The cheerful oval of his face grew serious. "I do not say she was not right, you understand. You are fortunate to be hardheaded, else no amount of skill or tending would have served."

"And I am in your home?" Still drawing challenging conclusions, I was.

"In Coloma." Then, seeing that the name struck no spark of recognition, he added, "About six miles north of Placerville. Eliza was dead certain that Doc Slapton would finish off what the blow had begun, so she insisted on my treating you."

"I am greatly in your debt," I said.

Dr. Richardson made a gesture of protest. "Sit still and be quiet; I want to examine you."

He made a great business of looking at my eyes; having me shut my lids then open each in turn while he watched the response of my pupils to the light. At last he was satisfied and remarked, "Your concussion has subsided. The bandage should remain for a few days, but you are on the mend. You will feel very stiff around the middle for a time, but thankfully no ribs are busted."

I had not even given any thought to my midsection.

"Is Miss Richardson here? I'd like to thank her as well."

Warning me again not to stand upright, he left the room and I heard the back door open. "Chin Lee," he called. "You gettee Missee chop-chop, okay?"

"Chinese," I sighed with relief. My hallucination was explained. "They were speaking Chinese."

"What's that?" the doctor said, returning to overhear my muttered comment.

"I said you have Chinese here."

Dr. Richardson laughed. "The Celestials? About a hundred in town. But only two of them work for me. Chin Lee is my gardener. His wife is my cook."

The wife of Chin Lee may have been the official household cook, but Eliza was wearing an apron and was dusted with flour up to the elbows when she entered my room.

"Well," she said by way of greeting. "You're still with us, I see."

I could not tell by this if she expected me to be down the road by now or dead. "I am most grateful . . ." I began.

She held up her hands. "You can see I'm baking half a dozen apple pies for the stage driver's wake. You got off lucky."

"Thanks to you, I am told."

She brushed me off like so much flour and addressed her father. "Funeral's in two hours, Dad. Will you be ready?"

The doctor rubbed his stubbled chin and glanced down at his rumpled shirt and trousers. "I am ready now, daughter."

"In a pig's eye. Ling is heating water for your bath. I've pressed your other shirt and mended your suit. It wouldn't hurt if you'd put your razor to a strop as well."

The old man grimaced. "Absence has not softened your temperament."

"Nor dulled my sense of smell. How long has it been since you had a bath? I've been away three years."

"You sound like your mother, may she rest in peace."

"If you traipse out to the cemetery without a bath you'll wake the dead and kill off a few of the living. That's a fact." She grinned and consulted me. "Mister Ryland, you have the look of an honest man. Tell my father the truth. It was not the whiff of home-cooked food that awakened you, was it?"

I did not enter into the family discussion, but I had indeed noticed that the smell of whiskey and sweat had grown stronger as the sun warmed the room. Doc Richardson indignantly hitched up his trousers and, mumbling like an unhappy schoolboy, scooted past Eliza.

With a wave of her hand she changed the subject. "Are you hungry?"

"I could eat."

"Flapjacks and bacon. I'll send Ling up with a plate directly." She turned as if to leave, paused a moment and said in a somber tone, "There's a posse out hunting the brigands who robbed our stage. The town is in a lynching mood. Nick Bledsoe leaves a widow and five kids behind. They've got an apple orchard down the road a mile. The kids will be in my classroom." She glanced up fiercely. "You're Wells, Fargo, aren't you?"

"I have a position in the San Francisco office when I get there."

"You'll see to it that Bledsoe's wife and kids are not left destitute, won't you?"

I started to tell her that I had no authority to promise anything, but thought better of it. I could not imagine that my new company would not see to the welfare of a widow and five children.

"Wells, Fargo takes care of its own," I replied importantly. "He was defending company property."

Satisfied, she nodded curtly. "I will hold you to your word, Mister Ryland." At that she left me abruptly to see to her apple pies.

Presently I was fed by Ling, the cook, who was a tiny Chinese woman of middle age wearing baggy trousers and a rough cotton tunic. At first, I mistook her for an adolescent male. I called her "laddie boy," at which she giggled and chattered in a dialect I could barely understand.

"Missy Eliza say Ling come feed skinny man. She say you too-starve like hound dog. All bones and ears."

So now I knew what the lady of the house thought of me. I rubbed a hand over my ribs and considered that I was, indeed, too long for my weight. My mama always said that one day I would grow up to match the size of my paws. My height stretched to six feet five inches, but I weighed only 165. Classmates at Princeton had dubbed me Ichabod Crane after I played the role of the lanky schoolmaster in the Sleepy Hollow Legend. This was a dark and terrible secret that I hoped to leave behind me. It had been my dream to come west and grow rich and fat. I had made a poor beginning of it.

Ling cut my flapjacks and bacon into tiny bits and attempted to spoon-feed me.

"No, thank you." Having a good set of teeth, I protested the dismemberment of my breakfast. "No need to cut it. I can chew just fine and feed myself, too."

My resistance infuriated the Oriental leprechaun. She wagged the spoon in my face and cried, "Eat! Eat! You skinny-bone man! Eat!" Humbled by this description and half afraid that Miss Eliza would come in person to scold me, I obeyed Ling and finished off my meal by her hand.

After this ordeal I slept a while until the sun shone full in the window and the solemn beating of a drum awakened me. A slight breeze stirred the muslin curtains, but the room was over-warm. I sat up slowly and swung my feet to the floor. I was dressed in a nightshirt that was much too short for me, but my trousers, clean and pressed, were folded on a chair as if Miss Eliza had expected me to be up and clothed when she returned from the funeral of Nick Bledsoe.

I dressed myself hurriedly, tucking the nightshirt into my waistband. My shoes were not to be found, and so I wandered barefoot through the house and out onto the broad front veranda. The Richardson dwelling was a neat, whitewashed house on a hill overlooking the town of Coloma. Grasping the porch railing and squinting down toward the main street, I was in hopes that I might glimpse the funeral procession.

From the high vantage point, I could see that the lanes were mostly deserted. A few Chinese stood silently waiting on the boardwalks of the business district as the boom of the drum was joined by the call of a bugle.

At the far extent of my view, behind the brick-and-plank buildings of Main Street, stretched the broad expanse of the American River. Just to the north were the remains of Captain Sutter's sawmill, where the first glint of gold had been discovered in January of 1848. I recalled the stories I read as a youth. When that momentous event took place a mere nine years before, the listening hills had been wild and unsettled. Who had not heard the tales of gold fever and tent cities built out of the sails of deserted ships left to rot in San Francisco Harbor?

Coloma had enjoyed perhaps a year of solitude after Sutter's employee, James Marshall, made his famous discovery, but that was all. Miners arrived by the tens, then the hundreds, and finally the thousands. The banks of the river and then the slopes of the hillsides were all dug, sifted, washed, and sorted. Eventually the river itself was turned from its bed so that the gravel on the stream bottom could be exhumed and examined.

In time the nearby placer claims played out, but Coloma advanced to an air of respectability. No longer a gold camp dependent on the cycle of boom or bust, Coloma became a supply depot for prospectors moving on to other strikes, other dreams. Those who made their fortunes in Coloma now were merchants, not miners.

Instead of a crude stockade, the jail was a solid stone structure in a clearing just beneath the Richardson house. Up the road on my left stood two churches and Miss Eliza's school. These institutions were a sure sign that civilization had come to the gold camp.

Shifting my gaze back down High Street toward town I could clearly read the signboards on the far side of Main: Bell's Store, the Sierra Nevada Hotel, a brewery, the Wells, Fargo office, a livery stable, and Wright's Hardware. On the near side of Main Street were the backyards and outbuildings of more hotels and saloons, and even a photograph studio.

Like a troupe of performers making a stage entrance, the black-plumed horses of Nick Bledsoe's hearse pranced onto the scene. The plain pine casket of the stagecoach driver was a stark contrast to the opulent black lacquer and gilt trim of the undertaker's wagon. A small, black-clad boy followed the hearse, beating a tattoo on a muffled drum draped in crepe. A large, florid-faced man in a top hat, boiled shirt, and formal suit was beside the child. This fellow carried the bugle, but on account of his dress, I took him for the undertaker.

Close behind came the widow; a mass of black fabric supported at the elbow by the parson. A tribe of small, ill-clad children followed her skirts like little ducks swimming after their mama.

At a respectful interval after the family, the townsfolk came into view. These good people were dressed in whatever they had handy to wear. There seemed to be several hundred of all shapes and ages and descriptions. At the head of the procession I spotted Doc Richardson and Eliza. The doctor looked considerably cleaner than at our first encounter. Eliza wore a white blouse and a black skirt. Different from the new fashion in the East, she did not wear her skirts full but dressed as though she might be going out for a ride or returning to work in her garden. She was a plain woman, I noted. Not beautiful, and yet there was something in the dignity of her posture that made her striking. Even at this distance I could see clearly that Eliza was angry and stricken at the senselessness of five children left without a father.

The mourners moved past the brick-walled store, a two-story hotel, and the brewery, then turned up the road by the Virginia Saloon. Then the hearse swung directly onto Brewery Street toward the church and the cemetery. It came to me that the entire population of the town would soon pass directly by my post on the veranda.

Glancing at my bare feet I turned to go inside the house when I spotted a group of riders entering Coloma from the opposite end of Main Street. At first I mistook them for stragglers who had arrived late for the funeral. Then I noted a hatless fellow bound and gagged on the back of a big buckskin horse. The posse had returned with a prisoner in tow.

I found my freshly brushed boots outside the back door and collected my laundered shirt from a clothesline; both courtesy of Ling, I imagined. I was moving more slowly than usual, but if I did not spin around suddenly, I no longer felt in danger of passing out.

By the time I had returned, shod and decently clad, to the veranda, the two cavalcades had collided. Just in front of the jail, there they were, all commingled together. The solemnity of the funeral cortege seemed to be abandoned.

My curiosity got the better of me and I crossed the yard and made my way down to the crowd. I was just in time to hear a mounted man say, "See here, Missus Bledsoe. We got the dirty skunk who killed your Nick."

The prisoner looked frightened, as well he might, because the line between grief and anger is thin at the best of times, and he was a very ready target. "I didn't kill anybody," he protested, his voice deep and rasping. I saw Eliza's head snap toward him when he spoke, and she frowned hard.

"You were part of the gang," the boastful captor said. "Accessory to murder is a hanging offense. Shoot, there's a fine limb on that oak over behind the jail. What do you say, Creedmore?" he addressed the undertaker. "Two for the price of one? Won't be but a minute's delay."

Two voices spoke in a sharp chorus of protest at this. One was Eliza's. "Tim Flynn," she scolded, "have you lost the little sense you were born with? This is a funeral. Look at how much pain you are causing. And there are children present, too! Jim, make him stop!"

Flynn looked abashed at her reproof, but what Eliza had said was mild compared to what came next. The figure addressed as Jim was a smartly dressed man with a high forehead, keen eyes, and fine, dark hair and moustache, and he was wearing a badge. "Be easy, Eliza," he said, "I'll handle this." It came to me of a sudden that there was more than just professional courtesy in his tone; something more personal. "Flynn," he said sternly and loud enough for all to hear, "I've had just about enough out of you. One more word and it'll be you I throw in the lockup."

"What for?" Flynn argued. He was trying to sound belligerent, but he was unconvincing.

"For inciting to riot," the deputy said. "Now I'm going to put the prisoner in the Coloma jail and there he will remain until his trial . . . his legally constituted trial, got it?"

I had not seen Ollie Turnipseed in the crowd before, but now his shining, bald dome pushed to the forefront. "Jim, I mean Deputy Hume, is it true that the prisoner was caught with some of the loot still on him?"

Once more the captive tried to argue with the accusation, saying something about it not even being his horse, but his voice was too low in volume to carry and he soon quit trying. Jim Hume allowed that Ollie's statement was correct. "But I'll have to keep the bullion as evidence," he said. "I'll give you a receipt for it."

"Not me," Ollie protested, "I'm just a guard. But there's a Wells, Fargo agent right there: Jack Ryland. And he may have something to say about treating this cutthroat too easy. This murderer, or one of his band, is who clobbered him. Nearly had *two* people kilt."

The next thing I knew, every eye in that crowd was fixed on me, or rather, on my bandaged head. I could feel a crimson flush crawl up to my scalp. "I was really just a passenger on the stage," I said. "My duties are in San Francisco. Isn't there a local agent who will take charge?"

It was Hume who answered me. "Claude Noteware is the Coloma agent, but he's away on business. I reckon you're elected till your company says different. Now we've held up the services long enough. Meet me at the jail afterward and we'll sort out who is responsible for what."

CHAPTER 3

The poet who said "Stone walls do not a prison make, nor iron bars a cage," had surely never seen the lockup at Coloma. The city fathers who planned the construction of Coloma's jail must have been expecting to imprison another Samson or a second Goliath. The stockade was built of stone, mortared into a single massive block of masonry. Though log cabins and shanties had been replaced by attractive buildings built of sawn lumber, the jug was by far the most substantial building in town. It surpassed even the brick store owned by a man named Bell; his walls bowed out and required timber bracing to keep them upright.

Moreover, inside the blockhouse were a pair of iron cages. Prisoners were further confined within these eight-foot cubes fabricated of riveted metal; to keep them from digging out with their dinner spoons, I suppose.

The only occupant of this dungeon was the man presented as Tom Baker. The narrow passage left between the cell and the stone wall was occupied by Deputy Hume and Ollie Turnipseed.

"I've appointed Ollie here to guard the prisoner," Hume announced. "Wells, Fargo will have to come up with another shotgun escort."

He spoke words with a challenging tone, as if daring me to argue with him.

I shrugged. "You are the law around here," I said. "I expect you can pretty much order whatever you want."

Jim Hume's eyes regarded me with a twinkle. I had five inches on him in height, but he stared up at my face with ill-concealed disdain. "What ever made you think you wanted to be an express company agent?" he inquired. "Most of the ones of my acquaintance are . . ." There was a pause while Hume groped for an appropriate phrase. "Most freight agents are of hardy stock; used to this country and the demands of the job."

I was determined to remain on good terms with the man. "Some misunderstanding," I explained. "I was hired by Wells, Fargo to work in the San Francisco office, not as a field agent. I'm an attorney."

Hume hooted, then recovered and said, "Aren't the hills of Frisco already populated with enough lawyers? You in charge of settling grievances or seizing the assets of the little freight businesses that Wells, Fargo takes over?"

I was aware of the fact that my new employer had driven many of its competitors out of business. Indeed, Adams Freight had only closed its Coloma office in the last year when it could no longer contend with Wells, Fargo. There was deep resentment in some circles. I shrugged and said, "Neither, actually. My training is in criminal law. Since the first stage robberies of a couple of years ago, Wells, Fargo feels the need to have someone to look after the company's interest during investigations."

"And you're it?" Hume guffawed. "Ollie, did you know that? Nothing like a little firsthand experience when starting a new job, eh?"

"Actually, I did not expect to be assigned a case on my own for several months," I said.

"Yeah? Well, you're up to your neck in this one! All right, enough chitchat. The prisoner here maintains that he is Tom Baker, that he has never before been south of the Yuba River, and that he found the buckskin horse wandering loose. He says he has no idea how the gold bars came to be in the saddlebags."

"All right," I said. "What next?"

"Well, look at him!" Hume fairly exploded. "Can you identify him as being in the holdup?"

I shook my head. "All but one of the robbers kept to the shadows. Their leader . . . the one who hit me . . . was about this fellow's height and build . . ."

"Go on," Hume urged.

"But," I said, wanting to be very careful not to put any man's head in a noose, "the bandits all wore hats and masks and long canvas coats. I could not make out the features of the chief. Was this man found with a slicker or some disguise on him?"

Hume grudgingly acknowledged the precision of the question. "No, but he may have discarded it as too incriminating."

"Then why not bury the loot if he could not get out of the area quickly enough? Surely gold bullion is more damning than an article of clothing."

The deputy regarded me with a small degree of respect. "That's just what I asked myself," he said. "Still, it seems clear from the broken reins that this man . . . or whoever the rider was . . . got thrown from the buckskin. Mayhap Flynn caught him just as he recovered the animal and before he could conceal the gold."

The prisoner, who had not been consulted though this conversation took place two feet from his nose, spoke up at last. "It's a dirty lie!" he growled.

Hume could tell by the sudden alert look on my face that something had struck me. "His voice," I said. "It's very like . . ."

"Like what?" Hume urged.

"The leader of the stage robbers has a voice that stuck in my mind," I explained. "He sounds like a young man, but his voice is roughened or thickened some way."

"Could you swear that the voice you heard and this man's are the same?" Hume asked, choosing his words carefully.

"Look at this," Tom Baker rasped, tearing open his shirt collar. An angry, red scar about half an inch wide encircled his throat. He croaked, "Flynn did this to me. I'm half hanged already. That's why my voice sounds like this!"

I turned back to see Jim Hume regarding me pointedly. At last I shook my head. "The voices are very alike," I said, "but I couldn't swear to it. What about Ollie? He was there, too."

Hume snorted. "Ollie told me about how forty brigands all carrying shotguns and broadswords assaulted the stage . . . but he couldn't recollect the sound of one man's voice!"

Ollie squeezed between me and the stone wall of the jail and scooted out the door. "It sure is hot," he announced. "I'll be right back. Just going over to the Metropolitan to wet my whistle."

"Make it lemonade," Hume ordered. "You're on guard duty, remember?"

The deputy and I watched Ollie out of sight, then both of us heaved sighs. "Not a credible witness," I said.

"Nope," Hume agreed.

"What about Miss Eliza?" I asked. "You should ask her to have a listen. She had more presence of mind than all the men on the stage."

"Doesn't surprise me," Hume interjected.

"Kept the bandit talking so as to memorize his tone," I continued. "What about asking her?"

"I already did," Hume acknowledged. "She said the same as you: couldn't be sure."

"You aren't gonna let me get lynched, are you?" the prisoner asked suddenly. "I seen the way the crowd looked at me. They want somebody to pay for killing the driver."

My eyes met those of Jim Hume. I like to think that both of us saw honorable intentions writ large. "You'll be moved to the county jail at Placerville to stand trial. Meantime, Ollie and Mister Ryland here will keep you safe."

"What about you?" I asked, following Hume out into the afternoon sunshine.

"Even if Ollie tends to exaggerate some, there's still at least six other robbers and the rest of the loot. I'll be back tomorrow or the day after." The deputy started toward his big bay horse, then stopped and turned to me. In a low but forceful voice he said, "And Ryland, let's be clear about one more thing. Eliza is Miss Richardson to you. I've been waiting for three years for her to come back west and she knows it. Now you do, too. See you keep it in mind."

When Ollie Turnipseed returned from quenching his thirst, he brought me a jug of lemonade as well. It was his way of saying that us fellow employees of Wells, Fargo needed to stick together. Pouring me a glass he said, "Jim Hume is a nice enough feller, but he takes his deputyin' right serious. Used to be a miner, same as regular folks, never hitting the big strike, but never quitting and going home, neither."

That information squared with my assessment of Hume: whatever else might describe him, weak-willed or quitter would not fit. I leaned the ladderback chair against a wall around the shady side of the jail and sipped lemonade. There was no need to urge Ollie to continue. "Got hisself appointed deputy about six months ago. Mostly he just collects taxes, hangs up notices, that sorta thing. But with Sheriff Carson down sick, Jim figures this is his chance to prove he's ready for more important duty. Figures a steady income goes with starting a family." Ollie looked at me significantly. He was given to blather and embellishment, but he was not completely without wits.

"Hey," a voice croaked from inside the lockup. "It's sufferin' hot in here. Any chance of a drink of water?"

I drained my glass, then refilled it and hollered, "How about some lemonade?" I carried the container in to Tom Baker and passed it through the iron lattice. He gulped it in one long pull, then grabbed his throat like the drink burned all the way down. I could not tell if the swallowing business was acting or not, but the look of gratitude he gave me when he passed back the glass seemed genuine enough.

Back outside Ollie said, "Almost forgot. The afternoon stage brought a message for you." He passed me a crumpled sheet of paper on which was scrawled an order from Wells, Fargo's headquarters. It confirmed what Jim Hume had already said: I was to take local charge of the investigation to see to the company's interests.

As I read the document it was clear to me that some idiot had assumed my training as a lawyer made me qualified as a lawman. I was charged with the task of organizing the capture of what was now called the "Tom Baker Gang." I could not imagine how I was supposed to accomplish such a task. My training instructed me to begin by acquiring a warrant for the arrest of persons unknown who were responsible for the holdup of the Wells, Fargo stage and the murder of Nick Bledsoe.

When I explained my plan of action to Ollie, he snorted in derision and exclaimed, "Now if I was you, which I ain't and I'm glad of it, I'd give out word a big gold shipment was enroute, then I'd stuff a coach full of keen-eyed duck hunters with double barrelled scatterguns who ain't afraid to kill a bad'n. Then when the Baker Gang come along and give the shout to stand and deliver, I'd let out a holler and deliver a load of buckshot where it counts."

"This is not the old days, Ollie," I admonished. "Law and order has come to the Sierra and I mean to go by the book and see that things are done properly."

At this Ollie slapped his knee and howled with laughter. "You gonna kill them desperadoes by throwing the book at 'em, are you? Make sure your aim is straight and the book is heavy. What they will throw back your direction will be a heap more lethal than leather-bound fancy words. Yessir, take more than a lawbook to kill these sidewinders."

I did not know what a sidewinder was. I admitted as much.

"You are green, ain't you, boy? It's a poisonous rattler what slides sideways across the sand. It'll come after a man when he don't see it comin', treacherous like, and it won't be stopped by nothin' but killin'. Can't threaten one, can't reason, can't coax, can't debate nor legislate with a sidewinder. As for warrants . . ." The old man crooked his fingers in a fanglike position and struck at me. I jumped involuntarily and Ollie howled with laughter again. "Reckon you aim to walk right through a nest of 'em, too."

I reddened at the insult, but asked him calmly to direct me to the acting legal authority in the county.

He scratched the stubble on his chin. "Placerville is the place to go. Used to be called Hangtown, but they changed the name since things got so respectable around these parts. Placerville's an hour's ride each way, down and back. 'Course, you ain't got no horse to ride. It's a sight farther when a man's afoot. Take you most of a day to go and come. Then mayhap you can rent a horse down to the livery. You do know how to ride, don't you?"

"In a town this size there has to be some legal authority," I responded, trying to get Ollie back on track. "This used to be the county seat before Placerville, right?"

It was the wrong tack to take. "Still would be if them Placervillians hadn't stole the election last time!" Ollie expounded. "Placerville paper said Coloma was cheating on the vote. Said there was certain irregularities. Can you imagine that? And here I been voting regular as clockwork . . . at least two or three times every election. What could be more regular than that?"

"Ollie," I said, holding up both hands to stop the torrent of words. "Local authority . . . who?"

"That'd be Judge Carl Dean Magee." Ollie wiped the tears of amusement from his eyes. "Leastwise he calls hisself a judge. Some rube in Sacramento appointed him to oversee disputes about mining claims and such. He set up shop down to the Metropolitan Saloon and Hotel so as to be close to his favorite mistress. Mistress Barleycorn. Magee is mighty fond of whiskey all right. He owns the saloon, too. But if you have to do this by the book and Placerville's too far to go, Magee'll be the one can sign the paper for you."

With the certainty that I was about to be the subject of the newest joke in Coloma, I left the jail. I was feeling discouraged as I headed toward the Metropolitan Saloon. Arriving outside the building on Main Street, I was startled by a rumble and a crash that seemed to come from beneath the foundation. Was there mining going on under the hotel?

Poking my head into a door at the bottom of a short flight of steps showed me the interior of the basement. There, in the cooler darkness below the inn was a three-lane bowling alley. A pair of half-drunken, bearded miners took turns attempting to knock over the ten pins at the far end of the wooden flooring. It was all that a pair of Chinese boys could do to avoid being mowed down while resetting the pins from the previous collision.

The Metropolitan was furnished at great expense in Victorian opulence. Shiny brass chandeliers hung from the high ceilings. A long, mahogany bar stretched from one side of the room to the other. A large oil painting of a naked woman lounging on a settee hung behind the bar. Red silk fabric covered the walls. It was plain that Judge Magee was a man of considerable wealth.

Letter of appointment in hand, I asked the whereabouts of the Judge's office. A heavyset Mexican bartender eyed me warily as he dried shot glasses. "You check your guns here, Señor. Don't nobody go up there with a gun."

I spread my hands as indication that I was unarmed. With a nod, the man jerked his thumb up the stairs.

There were two contrary images in my head of Judge Magee, and in the event, both were wrong. I hoped for a distinguished doctor of jurisprudence, with the lines of weighty decisions etched across his forehead. I would not have been surprised to find an expansive politician of expensive tailoring and impressive stature.

The man seated at the rolltop desk opposite the open door at the head of the stairs fit neither of these notions. "Judge Magee?" I inquired.

The bald-headed figure who pushed his leather chair back from the desk rose to a little above middle height. His head was not just sparse for hair; it was shaved, with all the impressive smoothness and sphericity of one of the below-stairs bowling balls. His was not an estimable physique either. His turn to face me was led by a paunch that drooped over his belt.

He regarded me without speaking with a pair of the coldest, most emotionless blue eyes I had ever seen. He wore his moustache long, drooping into a closely cropped imperial beard. The small triangle of whiskers looked absurdly out of proportion to the large round-ness of the head. But most startling of all was his age, or rather the lack of it. This man, assembled seemingly of spare parts, was no more than thirty years of age; not much older than me, in fact.

"Sorry to disturb you," I said. "I'm looking for Judge Magee."

"You found him," the man said. "State your busi-ness."

Magee remained standing, nor did he ask me to sit, though the room contained settee and side chairs. It was clear he did not expect the interview to last long. "My name is Jack Ryland," I said, extending my hand. Magee ignored it. I dropped it awkwardly to my side and explained my position with Wells, Fargo and my need for warrants.

"Out of my line," he said. "My jurisdiction covers mining disputes, water rights, and so forth. My time is far too occupied with matters of commercial interest to divert into criminal affairs. I could not get reimbursed by either the county or the state."

Magee was after payment. I stammered, "The sum stolen from the coach is considerable . . ."

Pouncing on my words like a fat cat on a slow mouse, Magee demanded, "How considerable?"

"Five thousand dollars in bullion, plus several hundred in coin."

"Have they posted a reward yet?"

"Not to my knowledge. There is also the matter of the murdered driver."

Magee dismissed the killing with a wave. "Can't be remedied now," he said. "Capture of the criminals and recovery of the stolen property . . . should be worth a thousand dollars, easy."

Did he mean offered as a reward or paid to him personally? "I'll have to consult my head office," I said.

Taking my statement as some sort of agreement concluded, Magee smiled a thin, brief smile, and said, "Of course you will. Now, I want to have a look at the man in custody. I'll fill out the papers and bring them to the jail. Shall we say in two hours then? Goodbye, Agent Ryland. Close my door on the way out."

I left the Metropolitan Saloon with an uneasy sense about my responsibilities. It was plain that no one in

Coloma thought I was up to the job assigned. I was inclined to agree with that conclusion.

After a turn around the town to get my bearings and draw some order from my tangled thoughts, I returned to the Richardson house. Ling was on the porch stringing beans for supper. Chin Lee worked diligently in his berry patch. Doc was out on a call.

"Is Miss Eliza at home?" I asked, pulling up a wicker chair beside Ling. It was hot and a pitcher of apple cider was on the table beside her. She paused long enough to pour me a drink.

"No, no. She gone to schoolhouse. She say when you come back you come schoolhouse, too."

"She wants to speak with me?"

"No, no. You speak her. Jim Hume come by and say you gonna die pretty soon you such a fool you don't even have no gun. I say I think you dead soon, too."

"And what did Miss Eliza say to that?"

"Missy Eliza want to know something important before you killed. Go to schoolhouse now."

I thanked Ling for her confidence in me, gulped back the cider, and headed for the school.

The Coloma schoolhouse was a one room white clapboard structure with three tall windows on each side. Climbing the steps at the front, I resolved to wait patiently on the porch until class was dismissed. Through the open doorway I spotted Eliza Richardson standing beneath a portrait of George Washington. She was reading to the pupils from a well-worn volume of

Charles Dickens's *Pickwick Papers*. I recognized the passage instantly as the one where Sam Weller reads his valentine aloud.

"There ain't nobody like you, though I like you better than nothin' at all," she intoned.

At that same instant, Eliza raised her eyes from the book and caught sight of my gangly frame. I felt myself color foolishly as though she had read Sam Weller's sentiment out loud and on purpose for me. Ling had made it clear that in the eyes of Miss Eliza I was only slightly better than nothin' at all.

I snapped off my hat and managed a smile. She paused in her recitation, glanced up at the clock, and then called for the class to come to attention.

"Ladies and gentlemen," she said in a dramatic voice, "tomorrow we shall continue with Mister Dickens. For now, however, please take out your readers and proceed with the lessons as I have outlined."

An audible groan rose up as the forty-some students obeyed her command.

Eliza crooked a finger in my direction, drawing me into her kingdom. Heads rose as I entered and passed down the aisle. She clapped her hands and warned that the lesson must be completed by the end of the hour.

In a whisper I greeted her. "Good afternoon, Miss Richardson." I remembered Hume's warning. "Ling gave me your message."

A question passed through her eyes. "I wished to congratulate you on your official appointment," she said.

"Thank you, Miss Richardson." I dared not look her full in the face. The news that she was to marry Jim Hume had made me even more awkward than usual. "I shall do my utmost . . ."

She interrupted. "I am certain you will remember your promise."

"My promise?"

"In regards to the Bledsoe family." She inclined her head toward the group of five children I had seen trailing the hearse. There was one boy, whom I guessed to be about the age of eleven, and four younger sisters.

"Indeed, I shall." I resolved to write the appropriate letter instantly.

Eliza had copied down the names of the children. Adam, Bette, Chloe, Danette, and Eve. "You see, from the youngest to the oldest they are each named in order with a letter. Missus Bledsoe told me yesterday that she and her husband had planned on getting at least halfway through the alphabet. But now, you see, things have gone wrong."

"I will see to the matter." I slipped the note into my pocket.

"And there is one more thing I wanted to speak to you about. I have grave doubts as to the identity of the prisoner. I cannot say for certain that he is one of the guilty parties."

I nodded. "I'm relieved you mention it. I had the same impression. I am leaning toward the belief that the posse picked up the wrong fellow."

"There is talk of lynching Tom Baker."

It seemed that the whispers had grown loud again as the day wore on. "Your Mister Hume will prevent that."

"My Mister Hume?"

"He seems a strong-willed fellow. Your fiancé will prevent violence from occurring, I have no doubt."

"My . . . what?" Her eyes widened in outrage at my statement.

"Mister Hume," I said in a very quiet voice since two dozen heads had bobbed up at the remark.

Eliza grabbed the sleeve of my coat and fairly dragged me back out onto the steps of the school. "My Mister Hume? Fiancé?" She tossed her head in defiance. "Whoever said such a thing?"

"Why this morning . . . Mister Hume said quite distinctly that . . ." My voice trailed off in intimidation of her brooding expression. I began again. "I take it no one has yet told you?"

"Bah!" She crossed her arms and glared down at the jail. "The impudence! Well! I will tell you something, Mister Ryland. I am the new schoolmistress. Replacing Miss Nellie Frankenviener who married Bump McConnell last week. Do you know what that means?"

"No, ma'am, I am afraid I do not."

"A schoolmistress in these parts is not allowed to be married. May not even have a beau. If that Jim Hume thinks he's going to make me lose my job so I'll be more inclined to say yes to him, then he'd better think again."

"Then you're not?"

"Well! The very idea!"

"I see."

"Good. Now that's settled. You tell that brute . . ."

"I'd rather stay out of it completely."

"Wise of you, Mister Ryland. No doubt he would blame you and you'd be thrashed again. I don't fancy sticking you back together a second time. Which is what I wanted to speak to you about."

"I have no intention of being thrashed again."

"Then you'd better get yourself a gun."

I blanched. "Would Mister Hume . . ."

"No! Not Jim Hume. It's your position I'm thinking of. Someone will kill you just for fun. You're Wells, Fargo after all."

"I am indeed."

"A sawed-off double-barrel shotgun will suit you. Bekeart's got just the thing in his gun shop. Seven dollars. Perfect for you, since you likely can't hit the side of a barn with something requiring aiming. Just point and squeeze the trigger. If it doesn't hit your target it will, at least, make a frightful noise. They will be made to believe you are serious."

"Thank you," I replied, though her remarks were nothing to be thankful for.

"Think nothing of it." She patted me on the shoulder in a sisterly fashion. "Hume may need another good man to help restrain the lynch mob if it comes to that. Nothing quite like a scattergun in such an hour. I know it must be difficult for a man your height, but don't forget to duck."

I thanked her again and replaced my hat. She bade me good day, promised to see me at supper, and instructed that if I had the aforementioned weapon purchased she would show me how to load it. At that she returned to her classroom while I beat a path for Bekeart's gun shop, where I purchased my shotgun, charged to Wells, Fargo, of course.

CHAPTER 4

After my meeting at the jail I moved into the agent's quarters at the Wells, Fargo office. Two things prompted my abrupt departure from the Richardson household: the first was Jim Hume's insistence that I was temporarily the official express company representative.

The other reason was also courtesy of Jim Hume. Whether or not he and Eliza had an understanding, I wanted no personal conflict to interfere with my work. The sooner I was out of Miss Richardson's care, the better Deputy Hume would like it. In any case, I had no excuse for remaining. Doc Richardson said for me to stop round the next day and he would examine the wound once more, but otherwise I was fit enough to shift for myself.

I found it strange that all the players in the stage holdup drama seemed determined to prove something: Jim Hume taking charge as sheriff, me in my new position with Wells, Fargo, even Eliza as brand-new schoolteacher and advocate for her charges.

The Wells, Fargo agency in Coloma was smack up against the Sierra Nevada Hotel on the east side of Main Street and the two buildings shared a common board-walk and canvas awning. Where the hostelry was two stories with a veranda and a string of second-floor rooms, the freight office was only a low stone-walled structure divided into two rooms. Facing the street side was an office with a counter, a desk, and a potbellied stove. At the back, behind a thin wooden partition were a cot, a blanket chest and the company safe. This black iron behemoth squatted in the corner of the room like a brooding pagan idol. The agent's living space had no window and no outside door, and the Wells, Fargo employee (in this case me) was the guard dog. At the moment there was nothing in the safe to guard.

I went to sleep that night to the clatter of dishes from the dining room next door. Drunken singing and laugh-ter from the Metropolitan across the street mingled with the rumble and crash of bowling balls. The combination made my cot bounce and filled my dreams, when I finally drifted off, with more of Washington Irving's sto-ries: Rip van Winkle and the elves playing at ninepins.

What woke me again was not a drop in the volume of noise, but a change in its tone. Before it had been bois-terous, but the mood it grew into was hostile and bel-ligerent. Through the curtain that separated the two halves of the office, I could see the flicker of torchlight coming from the street outside.

When my befuddled brain could sort the words from the angry drone, I heard cries of "Hang him! Drag him out now! Let's go get him!" mixed with mutters of agreement.

Hastily drawing on my britches, I hurried out the front door and locked it behind me. In the street I could see Tim Flynn on the front porch of the Metropolitan Hotel. He was tanked and slurring his words, but his harangue of the equally inebriated mob was effective. "Les' go get him, I say! What chance did he give Nick? Want to let some pettifoggin' lawyer get him off? Not on your life."

It was plain that the restraining effect Jim Hume had possessed over the crowd did not long outlast his departure. No one raised any question of fair trials or the rule of law or the possibility that Tom Baker might be innocent. The only objection I heard was a practical one: "How we gonna get him away from Ollie? I don't wanna get a load of buckshot in the face."

"You afraid of one old fool?" Flynn challenged. "How yeller are you?"

The consideration of Ollie as a guard would only hold them back so long, I knew. Soon enough Flynn's heckling and the amount of liquor they had put away would goad them to action.

I crossed the street behind the crowd, and when Flynn paused to draw breath I shouted, "And what will Jim Hume do to you, Flynn? And you other men, too?

Do you think no one will know you if you carry out this lynching?"

My thought was to head them off by making them worry about their own skins. Hume's forceful reprimand of Flynn had carried weight with the crowd. Perhaps invoking his name would work as well.

"Who's that speakin' there?" Flynn demanded. "Who's 'at thinks I'm afeerd of Jim Hume?"

The crowd parted, opening a corridor between me and Tim Flynn. "Agent Ryland," I said, trying to sound forceful and steady-nerved. "Men," I said, "what you're planning is not right and you know it. Lynch law is not justice, it's murder. You know what Jim Hume would say if he were here."

"Yeah," Flynn snarled. "Well, he ain't! And you are just the sort of shyster attorney I was talkin' about. We all knew Nick Bledsoe and liked him, and we all know that Baker feller is guilty as sin. Why should we hold back giving him what he deserves?"

During this speech Flynn had stepped off the porch and crossed the street until he stood just in front of me. I was much taller than he, and I tried to give my words a calming effect. "Because you don't know that he's guilty. You just want to punish somebody and he looks to be a likely candidate."

"Yeah?" Flynn murmured, as if actually considering my words. "Right now, there's one more likely than him!" With that he drove his fist into my midsection and I doubled over like a jackknife closing. Then he brought both hands together on the back of my neck and pummeled me face first into the dirt. "Action is what counts out here," he said, putting his boot on my head and grinding my nose into the street. "You're a weakling, Ryland," he concluded, turning on his heel and going back toward the saloon. "Weak and spineless. Go back east where you belong." Then in a mock whisper he added, "Keep out of my way or you'll get worse than this."

The crowd hurrahed Flynn's performance and accompanied him back into the Metropolitan for another dose of Dutch courage. Picking myself up, I smeared blood from my nose to the sleeve of my nightshirt, then plunged my head into a horse trough.

So much for reasoning with the mob. The only thing I had accomplished was to convince them that Flynn was right and anyone who spoke against him was feeble. If anything, I had reinforced his leadership by letting him prove that law did not rule above outraged sentiment.

I slipped along the shadows of the covered plank walkway until I came to the alley beside the blacksmith's. Ducking down to the river, I circled behind the row of buildings and popped out again farther along Main Street. My one idea was to warn Ollie about what was brewing. There might even be time to slip out with the prisoner and get him away to safety.

The thought that troubled me that night was this: What business was it of mine if some stranger got himself lynched? Why should I put my life on the line for someone I did not even know? What if he was guilty and deserved to be hanged anyway?

I thrust the disturbing notion away as forcefully as I could, because I knew the right answer. I had studied law because I believed in justice and the rules by which civilized men governed their affairs. Anyone was due a fair hearing, and not before a drink-crazed horde.

I hammered on the door of the jail. "Ollie!" I shouted. "Open up! It's me, Jack Ryland!"

"Mister Ryland?" Ollie questioned through the door. "What is it?"

"Flynn's got the crowd stirred up again," I warned. "They'll be coming soon. Let's move the prisoner now, before they get here."

"Where'll we take him?" Ollie argued. "If they catch us sneaking him out of town he'll swing for certain . . . maybe us, too."

"Hurry up," I urged. "Ollie, there is not time for this! They'll have you surrounded soon. We gotta get!"

"I dunno, Mister Ryland. Jim Hume told me to guard him. He didn't say nothing about taking him somewhere's else."

"Then turn him loose and let him make a run for it at least!" I could not believe what I was saying.

Then Eliza was at my elbow. By the light of the lantern she carried I saw she was in a dressing gown and slippers. "If he runs now they'll never believe he's innocent," she said. "I heard the noise of the crowd and guessed at what was up." She lifted the lantern, and the glow must have spilled across my swollen nose. Eliza gasped, but she did not stop to question what happened. "Ollie," she shouted. "Let Mister Ryland take the prisoner to Placerville. Hurry up!"

It was already too late. Around the corner of Brewery Street came a line of torches and half a hundred men. At their head was Tim Flynn and he waved them onward as though he were directing a cavalry charge. "I'll go get Reverend Pierce," Eliza exclaimed, and she handed me the lantern and sped off into the night.

"What about your father?" I called after her.

The words, "My father is . . . indisposed," came back on the breeze.

Flynn's shout of defiance reached me from across the field that separated the stone prison from Main Street. "Thought I told you not to interfere," he snarled. "You bootlickin' lawbook. Get out of the way or we'll make you wish you'd never been born."

Standing just to the side of the doorway I raised my voice to be heard over Flynn's tirade and spoke as if he were not even present. "Men," I said, "you are angry at the killer of Nick Bledsoe and you think Baker is the man. I'm here to tell you that Baker will not escape answering the charge. Ollie Turnipseed is inside the jail with the prisoner and he and I will see that Baker is kept safe for trial. Tom Baker will be tried. And if he's found guilty, he'll be punished, but not this way."

"Outta the way, milksop," Flynn said, advancing toward me. "You ain't no more than what I wipe off my boots."

The spy-through hole opened in the center of the oak door and Ollie Turnipseed shoved the shotgun barrel out. "That's far enough, Tim Flynn," he called. "Jim Hume give me the job of guardin' this pris'ner, and he ain't goin' nowhere."

"Let's rush him," Flynn said to the crowd back of him. "Bust the door down."

"Sure, Tim" one of his friends said. "You go first."

"Look," Flynn said and cursed. "We got torches, see? We go back of the jail where he can't shoot nobody and we light up the roof. Either he gives us Baker or they both fry. What about it?"

"That'll be enough of that!" came a shout from the hillside back of the prison. It was the preacher, Reverend Pierce, returning with Eliza. "You men break this up at once, do you hear?"

"Keep outta this, Parson," Flynn warned. "This don't concern you."

"How many of us will you say that to, Flynn?" Pierce challenged. "Mister Ryland and Ollie and Miss Richardson and now me? Will you kill us all? Because I swear to you, we will have you up on a charge of murder if you do this thing you intend."

From inside the jail came a nervous outburst in the guttural tones of Tom Baker. "Don't let 'em hang me, Parson! I ain't ready to meet my Maker!"

"Do you hear that, Flynn?" Pastor Pierce demanded. "Do you want this man's eternal fate on your conscience?" Raising his voice he continued, "What about you others? Are you willing to send an unprepared man to his death?"

"What about Nick?" Flynn retorted. "What chance did he have to get ready to go? That killer never give Nick a chance . . . why should Baker get one?"

"I'll answer for the condition of Nick Bledsoe's soul," the preacher stated bluntly. "He knew his Lord and was ready to meet Him. But what about you, Tim Flynn? What if you were in this cell expecting to be dragged out and hauled up a tree limb? Is your conscience so clear? What about you, Helms? Or you, Mackleroy? Or you, Simmons?"

The preacher looked round the group of men, calling them each by name; calling them to reckon themselves in the place of the accused, facing an untimely end. I saw it happen. There were still fifty men standing in front of me, but it was no longer a mob. Instead there were fifty stripped bare individuals.

"Every one of you will face the Great Judge someday," Pierce continued. "What will you say when the spirit of Tom Baker accuses you of this night's horror? Evans, how will you excuse yourself? Josh Briscoe, what will be your answer?"

The preacher had them then. Flynn had lost them and he knew it. "If Baker has something on his conscience it must be 'cause of murderin' Nick," Flynn said, trying to regain the weight of opinion. He was too late.

"Hold on, Tim," Helms said. "Parson is right. This ain't no way to go."

"Are you all yeller?" Flynn snarled. "I'll drag him out myself, then!" Encouraged by some angry muttering, he took two steps toward the jail. Ollie raised the shotgun but the preacher waved for Ollie to lower it again.

Then Reverend Pierce lifted what he had in his hands. It was not a Colt Navy or a twelve-gauge greener, but a battered old leather-bound Bible. "If you are willing to kill me to get to the prisoner," Pierce said, "then come ahead. But you will listen to what I have to say first. I was in Old Dry Diggings in '49." He stopped there and let his words sink in. The date and place had no significance for me, but several in the crowd shuffled their feet nervously.

"Many of you know what I'm going to tell," Pierce continued. "I wasn't a preacher then, but I was there . . . I was there when three men who had been whipped for stealing were accused of still another crime . . . and hanged by a drunken mob." His voice broke and his head drooped. "I watched those three men hanged . . . lynched! And I made no move to stop it, because everyone said they were guilty and that made it so, didn't it? And when they spoke no words in their own defense, that confirmed their guilt! And do you know what I found out the next day? You, Simmons, you know! What was it?"

The man addressed as Simmons rubbed a dark bandana over a pale and downcast face. When his mumbled reply could not be heard, Pierce answered for him: "What we found out the next day was that all three hanged men were foreigners, who spoke no English! They could not even raise a cry of protest that could be understood, and no one took their part! Never again." Pierce concluded, "I have the faces of those men before me in my dreams . . . I have their blood on my conscience to this day and will carry it to my grave! But I will *not* stand by and ever let it happen again!"

There was a stillness so complete that the bubbling gurgle of the river a quarter mile away was plainly heard, but nothing else. "Then come on, if you've still a mind to," Pierce said quietly to Flynn. "All you have to do is kill me first."

The tail end of the crowd was already drifting away, back toward the saloons or to their bunks. Tim Flynn stood clenching and unclenching his fists, 'til two of his friends took him by the elbows. He shook them off angrily. He divvied a last glance of pure malice between the pastor and myself, then turned and walked away.

CHAPTER 5

My new position came with a small stipend of thirty dollars a month, which made me among the poorer residents of Coloma. I comforted myself with the realization that since I had lost my father's watch I had nothing left to make me a target for robbers. Along with the salary, the company provided two meals a day taken at the Sierra Nevada Hotel next door.

Although located beside the brewery on its other face, the hotel was a temperance establishment. Lack of beer and hard liquor at the table meant that the Sierra Nevada attracted a quiet and genteel clientele. This suited me right down to the ground.

It was a couple of mornings after the near lynching. I was just handing the proprietor, Mrs. Nichols, my company meal voucher when the clatter of hooves and the rapid firing of a revolver outside interrupted.

Unmindful of stray bullets I stupidly went out on the porch to gawk. Mrs. Nichols, a large, homely, miner's widow shouted to me not to be such a fool, but I ignored her.

Two Mexican riders wearing broad-brimmed sombreros and silver-studded chaps galloped past the hotel. They reined up outside the Wells, Fargo office, swung off their scruffy ponies and pounded on the door!

"Señor Ryland! Señor Ryland!"

Remembering my beating and half-afraid that the other members of the outlaw gang had unaccountably decided to finish me off, I hesitated a moment in hopes of learning what business they wanted with me.

"Jack Ryland!" The shorter of the two men tapped against the glass of the window and called, "Wake up! Are you in there, Señor Ryland? We have ridden from Georgetown! Señor! There has been another holdup! The Georgetown stage!"

I did not have breakfast that morning. The two riders had come looking for the new Wells, Fargo agent at the request of the Georgetown constable. The stage between Georgetown and Volcanoville had been stopped and robbed a mile outside his jurisdiction. No one had been killed, but the makeup of the gang sounded similar to that of the robbers who had killed Nick Bledsoe. Being as the crime was committed against another Wells, Fargo shipment, this was a matter for a Wells, Fargo agent to handle. I was the nearest at hand. There were passengers willing to give me depositions and descriptions if I would ride to Georgetown before the next stage took them on the next leg of their journey.

It seemed urgent that I respond. "How long will it take to reach there?"

"A few hours, no more," explained the short man. "My brother and I will ride with you. Saddle your horse. We will eat and then we must go quickly."

The brothers retreated to the Sierra Nevada Hotel to eat my breakfast while I set out to borrow a mount.

I hurried to the livery stable. Jethro Creedmore, the florid-faced undertaker, was also owner of the livery stable. Still in his red flannel long handles and looking much less dignified than the day of the funeral, he opened the barn door and squinted out at me.

"You're the new feller. Wells, Fargo, ain't you?"

"I need a horse," I said urgently. "Wells, Fargo business. A holdup over Georgetown way."

He rubbed the stubble on his cheek. "Cain't give you a coach horse. Got a worn out six-up team due in at three o'clock this afternoon. I'd lose my contract if'n I lent out a fresh horse to somebody."

"But I am Wells, Fargo," I drew myself up importantly. Mr. Creedmore was not impressed.

"Sorry. It takes a six-up team to pull a Concord coach. Five won't do it. Cain't let nobody take one of the team."

In the gloom behind Mr. Creedmore I could see the wide, strong back of the buckskin horse that had been captured with Tom Baker. "There. I'll have to ride the buckskin. Caught in a Wells, Fargo robbery. Must be company property."

Creedmore scratched his belly and shook his head slowly from side to side. "Naw, sir. Over Jim Hume's dead body. Which means Hume would kill me if I let that there horse out of this barn. That there horse is evidence, that's what he is."

"I'll rent a horse from you, Mister Creedmore."

"I don't rent horses to Wells, Fargo employees. Had one returned lame and never did get paid for it."

"Then I'll have to buy one."

"You pay cash on the barrelhead?"

Frustration was mounting. I considered my meager salary and the state of my finances. "Wells, Fargo will pay."

"Naw, sir. Cain't do business thataway no more. Wells, Fargo is always way behind. You know how much they owe me? Two months on feed, and hay is two hundred and fifty dollars the ton. What if they go out of business? Then I'm high and dry with horses I cain't hardly give away."

"I need a saddle horse," I said firmly. "Now."

"You need a saddle, too? That'll cost extra."

I made a quick mental calculation. "I have twenty-three dollars cash." I should not have told him what I had in such exacting detail. The wheels of his greedy brain began to spin as he considered what animal he could get shed of and make twenty-three dollars.

He shrugged and stepped aside, allowing me into the barn. The hearse was parked beside a buckboard. Pine coffins leaned against the wall. "I might can help you.

Come on then." He did not bother to dress, but led me past the stalls where handsome, well-broke horses stood serenely munching hay. Out the back door were two corrals. Each held a half dozen animals. They were decent-looking. Not knowing much about horseflesh, I was encouraged.

"These just come in yesterday. Carson Valley horses they are. Take a bit of ridin' out, but any one of them will gentle down for you."

"Riding out? Gentle down?"

"Well, they're green broke, if you know what I mean."

I nodded as if I knew. My mind clicked off possibilities. Green? Hadn't Eliza called me green? And then Ollie repeated the insult. If it was true for me, what did it mean when a horse was green broke? Unripe, sour, bitter, and likely to turn my stomach if I bit off more than I could chew.

I replied, "I need a horse I can ride today."

Creedmore clapped his hand warmly on my back. "You can ride any one of these horses today. Ride 'em out, I say! Take that one there." He pointed to a jug-headed roan. "Take a look at the slope of that shoulder. Pure power. By the time you get back he'll be gentle as an old dog."

As if to dispute Creedmore's accolades the roan delivered a cannonlike kick to the sorrel standing behind him. Nostrils flared and ears laid back, he then charged toward the section of fence where we were standing. Creedmore leaped back. I did likewise.

Creedmore wiped his hands on the front of his flannels and chuckled nervously. "Mebbe not that one. But any one of the others."

I was green as grass, but I was not altogether ignorant. It occurred to me that one of these creatures was much like another. If I rode out on one of Creedmore's brutes, I might well be the next customer in his undertaking business.

"I'm no fool, Mister Creedmore," I said. "I haven't got the time."

"You ain't got the money, neither, son. But I'll tell you what I'll do. I got me a well-broke mare in there in the barn. Fine animal. All the manners anyone could want. Collected her off an actor in payment of a feed bill. Her name is Ophelia."

I held up my hand to silence him. "She has a name?"

"'Course she has a name. That actor feller thought highly of her, too. He was sorry to give her up, I'll say. But he owed me a debt. Hay is two hundred fifty a ton . . ."

"So you said."

"And this mare et a ton."

"I'll have a look."

At this, Creedmore began to qualify his praise of Ophelia. "She don't look like much. I put her to pasture over the winter on account of she cost me so much already. She's been foraging like and ain't got the meat on her like these others." Swinging back the barn door he gave a sharp whistle. "Ophelia, darlin'," he crooned.

A soft nicker sounded from the third stall to the right. A moment later the white face of a paint mare appeared and bobbed a greeting. She had one blue eye and one as soft and gentle brown as a Jersey cow. Her ears were pert and her lower lip drooped and quivered as she nickered once again. I stroked her velvet nose. It was love at first sight. Only I should have seen the rest of the package before I committed to marriage.

Creedmore grabbed up the pitchfork and flung a load of poor hay over the gate. "She's a sweet one, is Ophelia. You cain't go wrong with her."

"I'll need a saddle and a bridle as well." I was not much good at bargaining.

"I'll make you the loan of her saddle and bridle, but I got too much in this fine mare to just give away everything. Twenty-three dollars? You're stealin' her from me, that's what. Kinda hate t' let her go. She's sure good company. Gentle as an old dog. There's a feller up Auburn way has spoke an interest in her."

Ophelia nickered gently from her stall as she browsed the hay. It was as if she was speaking to me.

"All right. I'll take the saddle on loan."

"Leave her to finish her breakfast. We'll settle up in the office."

His office was a rolltop desk inside a stall. Creedmore's trousers hung on a nail above his cot. I dug into my pocket and counted out my last cent. Whereupon the undertaker/horse trader presented me with a bill of sale that described my horse in detail.

PAINT MARE. NAMED OFEELYA. SORREL WITH WHITE BELLY. FOUR WHITE SOCKS. BALD FACED. LEFT EYE BLUE. AGE UNKNOWN. SOLD TO JACK RYLAND THIS DAY.

I frowned a bit at the part that said, AGE UNKNOWN. I should have asked about that before I paid. I asked as we walked back to her stall.

"Age?" Creedmore inhaled, as though sniffing the air might give him some clue. "It's hard to tell. I'd say she's about six. Give or take. Put a little hay down her gullet and she'll look like a little filly again. Guaranteed."

He swung back the gate and for the first time I got a full look at what my twenty-three dollars had purchased.

Creedmore had already collected. He had no reason to be encouraging, but he attempted to ease my concerns all the same. "Like I said. A little hay . . ."

"A little!"

"Feed her molasses in her grain. That always does it. She'll pick right up. An easy keeper, Ophelia."

My mare looked old enough to have voted . . . for Andy Jackson. Behind that pretty face was a bag of bones. The cost of feed came to mind. By the time I poured enough hay down her scrawny throat to change her looks from scarecrow to horse I would be riding a thousand-dollar animal.

Creedmore slipped a loop around her neck. She balked when he attempted to lead her from the stall. "She don't want to leave her feed, that's all." He whacked her on her boney rump and she lunged out of the cubicle.

I hopped out of the way as she snorted and stamped and attempted to go back in.

"You sure I can ride her today?" What had I done?

"She's the horse for you, son. Just you fetch me that feed bag."

I obeyed. He slipped the bag over her nose and Ophelia calmed down. I looked her over. I felt queasy. I queried in a halting voice, "How long will it take her to . . . fill out?"

Giving her a quick curry, Creedmore replied, "Guess that's up to you. Depends how good you treat her, don't it?"

He slipped the saddle on her back. It was a U.S. Cavalry saddle. Light and basic. Hard as a stone. Leading her out of the barn before he slipped the feed bag off, Creedmore was humming softly and happily as he handed the reins to me.

I mounted. Nudged Ophelia. She backed up.

"You gotta show her who's boss," Creedmore shouted.

I kicked her. Not hard enough.

The Mexican brothers from Georgetown rode around the corner. They rested easy in their saddles and sucked their teeth as I urged Ophelia away from the barn.

The short brother called to Creedmore. "So. You got rid of *caballo vieja* at last, eh, amigo?"

Creedmore chuckled and retreated into his dusty sanctuary. He emerged a moment later with a large kettle and a hammer. With a whoop, he banged the hammer against the kettle like a drum. Ophelia reared up, whinnied, and galloped out onto the main street of Coloma as the Mexicans cheered. I heard one of them call after me, "Señor Ryland! Georgetown is the other way!"

The trail to Georgetown was well marked and the town only about ten miles distance from Coloma. My destination sat atop the Divide, the high ground that separated the middle and south forks of the American River. It would not have been a long journey at all, apart from the fact that between Coloma and Georgetown there was a gain of some two thousand feet in elevation. Ophelia seemed not to have any unexpected reserve of speed, so I resigned myself to travelling at her plodding pace.

At one point climbing a grade up a long rocky slope, we were moving so slowly that I stepped off the mare's back, believing that we could make the ascent faster if I led her. Turned out I was wrong, and at the next plateau I climbed back aboard.

Juan, the younger of the two Mexicans, reined his horse back to me for the dozenth time in the last half mile and waited as I mounted. "Perhaps, señor," he said politely, "you would like for us to ride ahead and tell them you are coming?"

I agreed that such might be a good idea. "Unless I need you to guide me," I pondered aloud.

"Oh no, señor," Armando, the elder, said hastily. "The road, she is plain enough. Do no turning and you will arrive safe."

By *tomorrow* he probably thought of adding, but in consideration of my feelings, left it unsaid.

"Then good enough, gentlemen," I agreed. "You go on . . ."

I had not finished what I was going to say when with a spurring touch of five-inch-wide rowels they whirled and were gone. I was left to my thoughts and the climbing road and the company of Ophelia.

The highway to Georgetown crossed ravines down which I glimpsed miners at work on their claims. I also passed the wooden frameworks of flumes, looking like timber centipedes crawling over the slopes. Certain enterprising types, finding it too hard to earn a living from gold panning were turning water into gold. By damming streams in the high mountains and channeling it through flumes to the dry canyons, they allowed the washing of gold to proceed in places where it had been nearly impossible; for a price, of course.

A snake crawled across the road in front of me, paying me no regard at all. I looked him over good to see if I could determine any of the characteristics of a sidewinder, but he did not hold still for close inspection. Just as well, probably. I also thought I caught a glimpse of a bear ambling down a gully. At first glance it appeared to be a particularly hairy and ungainly cow, but reflection changed my mind.

What a country! Snakes and bears and outlaw bands, renegade men and renegade horses, all set amid miles of silence and picturesque desolation. Yet for all the lonely feel, the signs of civilization were coming to the Divide. A hillside across the way was dotted with the regular-spaced plantings of an orchard. It was too far to see what the small trees were, but I guessed them to be apples. Recently planted, too, being not more than three feet tall.

This was a land of possibility. A man could grow up with this country. If he had a good woman by his side. Eliza Richardson was such a woman: practical, capable, and self-confident. She was much in my thoughts along the road.

That was when I heard the scream. I had not then been informed about the listening hills, and the woman's voice shrieking in terror seemed to come from just over the next ridge.

I set my spurs to Ophelia; that is, I clapped her ribs with my heels harder than usual. She stirred up dust with her front feet . . . once . . . before returning to her normal amble.

We crested the rise and I reined her to a stop. She was so surprised that she actually continued forward a few paces before stopping to gnaw her lower lip. I stood upright in the stirrups (which was a pleasant change from the army saddle anyway) and surveyed the landscape.

There were no distressed females that I could see. In fact, I could not make out any human presence at all. Then I heard it again. Definitely a cry for help, and it came from south of the road and up a little draw set at right angles to the main canyon.

Nudging Ophelia forward, I got her up to a trot on the downhill plunge. About halfway along the slope it came to me that I did not know what I was riding into. Moreover, whatever it was, I was hardly prepared to deal with it. In my haste to leave town, I had forgotten my newly purchased shotgun. Just as well; as unpracticed as I was, I was more danger to myself. So: no coach gun, no rifle, no pistol, no firearm of any kind. In short, I was without the preferred method of dealing with trouble in this part of the world.

I would have to improvise, then. From the screams that still came at irregular intervals from the dry wash up ahead, I was at last certain of the location. I turned

Ophelia aside and forced her up a line of rocks, through thorny brush covered in yellow flowers.

Ophelia sneezed. Boney and swaybacked though she was, my mount produced a prodigious noise that I was certain would give me away.

Swinging out of the saddle, I tied her to a small oak. Next I clambered up a narrowing rocky ledge on foot, 'til I could look down into the gorge on the other side.

There below me was a small two-wheeled cart in a clearing beside a thin trickle of water. A beautiful young blonde-haired woman stood with her back to an oak tree. At her feet crouched a white-haired man dressed in a fringed buckskin suit, holding a long-barrelled rifle.

Man and woman looked toward the mouth of the canyon as if expecting danger from that direction. When I turned my gaze that way, into view hurdled a savage Indian. He wore a full bonnet of bright-colored feathers, war paint, leather leggings, and he brandished a tomahawk that gleamed as he twirled it round his head.

The murderous aborigine sprinted across the intervening yards. I saw the man in buckskin raise his weapon and take aim, but it must have misfired, for no crack of a gunshot reached me. He reversed the rifle then, to use it as a club.

The defender of the woman swung once at the Indian's head, but the savage ducked under the blow. Another sweep of the rifle aimed at the attacker's legs, but the brave adroitly jumped over the arc, crashing into the man in buckskin. The hatchet was raised to strike.

Through this assault the blonde woman gave shriek after piercing shriek, yet made no move to assist in her own defense. Weaponless or not, I had to do something! Jumping to my feet, I raised a fiercesome yell of my own, hoping to make the noise convince the Indian that a whole troop of cavalry was coming to the rescue.

I did better than I intended, for partway down the descent, my feet lit on a patch of loose gravel and my charge turned into more of a plunge. A rock slide started on both sides of me, and suddenly my dash was accompanied by bounding boulders and rolling limbs of dead wood.

The buckskin-clad man had grabbed hold of the Indian's upraised tomahawk and they rolled over and over on the ground, striving for possession of the blade. At the noise of my onslaught, both turned to face me and their eyes grew wide. They got to their knees, still wrestling for the hand ax.

The woman's screaming turned more shrill, before ending in a high-pitched squeak. She jumped into the bed of the wagon and brought out a shotgun.

I had just a second to wonder why she had not used the scattergun before when a load of lead pellets blew the tops off a clump of manzanita just six feet to my right. She was shooting at me!

There was no way to stop or turn back. It was all I could do to keep my legs churning fast enough for my feet to remain under me. In the final sprint I cannoned into attacker and defender both, bowling them over and fetching up against the wheel of the wagon.

Grabbing the tomahawk, I wrenched it free and held it threateningly over the Indian's head. "Don't move," I said with menace, "or I'll split your skull wide open. Uh . . . Injun understand?"

"Bravo!" The buckskin-wearing frontiersman applauded. "Oh, good show! Would you be so kind as to let me up now?"

He sounded extremely unperturbed for one who had been near to death a moment before. Then he added, "You really should get your knee off Frank's chest, too. I do think he's having difficulty breathing. And Tess, put that weapon away before you hurt someone."

When I lowered the hatchet and looked into the bloodthirsty savage's face, he was as much a paleface as me! Light-complected, but flushed from being out of breath, the man I had disarmed was short, fair-haired, and plump.

"What is this?" I said as I stood up and dusted myself off. "I heard the lady screaming from a mile away."

"Yes," the white-haired man agreed. "Amazing acoustics, really, these listening hills. I've told Tess she should keep the volume down when we rehearse, but she gets caught up in her striving for realism."

"Rehearse?" I said stupidly.

"How silly of me," the white-haired figure said, extending his hand. "Of course, you thought this was genuine. My goodness, Frank, what a compliment." The man named Frank stood up slowly, rubbed his ribs and brushed himself off. "My name is Tyrone Hampton," the white-haired man continued. "The troupe is named after my humble self as the founder. This is Frank Crowley and our damsel in distress is Tess Darby."

"Charmed," the young woman said. On closer inspection she was in fact blonde, but not as young as she had first appeared, nor as beautiful. Her hair being worn in long ringlets had confused me.

"We are rehearsing a new playlet to add to our repertoire," Tyrone explained. "*The Cabin in the Woods,* or *Last of the Mohicans.* You are familiar with James Fenimore Cooper?" I nodded dully. "Splendid! The bandages are extremely well thought of. Wounded hero and all that. Are you free to begin rehearsing at once? Our first performance is in two days."

"Perform, where?"

"Georgetown, of course. That's where the rest of our cast is right now, Lavinia and the others, making advance bookings and parading around in costume to drum up business."

That was my first encounter with the Hampton Theatrical Company. I said good-bye to the maiden and the

Indian. Tess fluttered impossibly long eyelashes at me and said I was a gallant gentleman to come bare-handed to the rescue of a stranger. Frank also muttered something under his breath, but I missed it.

Tyrone Hampton walked along with me to retrieve my mount and explained the troupe's presence in El Dorado County. "I'm English, you see," he said. "I was playing Shakespeare in the theaters of the East . . . Washington, New York, Philadelphia . . . to, if I may say, favorable notices, when I heard of the gold strike. That was enough for me. I saw a golden opportunity to own my own business and around the Horn I came." He went on to describe how he had been putting on shows in gold rush towns for the last seven years. At first he had done solo acts, soliloquies from *Hamlet* and the like, but had gradually expanded his company to its present eight-person cast. "We perform drama and tragedy as well as high and low comedy," he said, adding drily, "with ever an eye to the tastes of our clientele. Many a suicide scene from *Romeo and Juliet* has been interrupted with shouts of 'Don't do it!'" He shook his head. "Ah, the responsibility of bringing culture to this savage land. But at least our performances are well attended. That's very flattering to the actors, even if there is an element of danger involved."

"Danger from bandits?" I asked, thinking of the two holdups that I was supposed to be investigating. I was not making much progress along that line. "Sidewinders?" I added knowledgeably. "Bears?"

"Nothing like," Tyrone corrected. "Audiences."

"You mean they turn mean if they don't like the production?"

Tyrone drew himself up proudly. "My dear sir," he scolded. "There is never an occasion when we do not render our craft to the highest standards! No, it's their approval of which I speak."

I was well and truly confused. "You said, danger."

"Egad, sir, remember Juliet with her dagger posed? Remember your own response to Tess's screams? [How could I forget?] Think what happens when it appears to five hundred inebriated miners that Frank as a bloodthirsty Iroquois is near to scalping me! Gunshots! General melee! Actually lost a partner that way once . . ." His voice trailed off in remembrance, then he shrugged. "Ah, well, the treading of the boards has never been an easy lot. We now insist that the patrons be disarmed at the door, but some of them have astonishingly accurate pitching arms with tumblers of whiskey and the like."

I was relieved to find that other onlookers had also been gulled into responding as if the scene enacted were real. Of course, my consolation evaporated quickly when I recalled that the other dolts had the excuse of drunkenness.

The subject then turned to my own arrival out west and my unexpected employment as a lawman. Since the Hampton Company travelled throughout the region, I asked if they had taken any notice of strangers riding in canvas slickers in the past week. He indicated that the company had been north, up Nevada City way. They had heard of the robbery and the killing of Nick Bledsoe, but had no information to offer. "We shall certainly keep our eyes open," he offered. "Are you certain that you don't wish to throw over your mundane vocation for a chance at fame on the stage?"

I told him that one stage mishap at a time was enough for me, but I do not know if he saw the humor in my remark. He said, "A pity. There is something about height and conformation. It puts me in mind of something, if I can just recollect . . ."

Fearful that he was going to dredge up *The Legend of Sleepy Hollow* from his memory, I hastily said, "Well, now. Here's my horse. Imagine I'd better be getting along before they send a search party back after me."

Tyrone stared at my horse. Even before he spoke, I knew what he would say. "You say *this* is your animal. But there can't be two . . ."

"Ophelia," I agreed, wishing myself able to disappear and leave both horse and actor behind. "How old was she when you traded her to Creedmore?"

"She was a loyal and faithful companion of . . . many years. I would never have parted with her except because of extreme financial embarrassment. Why Mister Ryland, her bloodlines go back to those of the mounts of the conquistadores!"

"Spare me the condolences, Mister Hampton," I said. "All I care is that she is not herself one of the horses used by the conquistadores."

With that we parted. He suggested that if I contacted Lavinia in Georgetown, she would give me a complimentary ticket to the next performance. I had no mind to tell anybody the circumstances of my encounter with the actors, but merely said I would not be staying in Georgetown long enough to attend. "A pity," Tyrone concluded. "Another time, then."

CHAPTER 6

Georgetown proved to be a very civilized village of about five hundred souls. Even though it was located farther up in the mountains than Coloma, the days of log cabins and tents seemed ended there as well. A sign greeting my arrival read: HENRY JACOBS, DEALER IN BOOKS AND STATIONERY. Of course the advertisement went on to elaborate that Mr. Jacobs also dealt in cigars, wallpaper, cutlery, candy, and kerosene, but what was wrong with finding all one's needs met by one stop?

My Mexican messengers had instructed me to go to the offices of the Citizens' Accommodation Line Stage, easily located at the Union Hotel. There I found Juan and Armando, who appeared extraordinarily pleased at my appearance. Apparently they were in some trouble for having returned without me. "Señor Ryland," Armando said with evident relief, "this is Señor Parker of the stage company and this is Señor Hussey, the constable."

Constable Hussey showed himself to be a no-nonsense, take-charge sort of man. "Where have you been, Ryland?" he demanded. "We expected you an hour ago."

"Followed up a promising lead," I said, having worked out my excuse on the way. "Met an acting troupe camped beside the road and interrogated them. Could turn up something . . . you never know."

Parker was willing to accept my explanation, but Hussey was still vexed. "See here, Ryland," he said, "we had to let the passengers and driver go on. Couldn't keep them cooling their heels here any longer."

The down stage must have passed me on the road while I was saving Tess from the Iroquois war party. Best to get done here as soon as possible and get back out of town before the actors compared notes.

"I see," I said evenly, annoyed with myself and trying not to show it. "Did someone take depositions?"

"Right here," Hussey allowed, waving a sheaf of papers. "You can take 'em to read over, but I'll give you the gist. Stage was stopped between here and Volcanoville last night. Men in masks and slickers jumped it from behind a roadblock. Nobody can describe nothin'."

"What was the take?"

"Strongbox had about a thousand in gold. Passengers lost jewelry and pocket money. It's all writ down there."

"You send out a posse?" I asked.

Hussey grunted. "Every young buck who figured to take time off from his claim or his job is already riding with one of Hume's groups. Who's left to send?"

"Yes, I see," I responded. "Has Hume been notified?"

"Sent another rider after him, but heard he was away south of Placerville. May take another day to get organized."

Parker broke in at that point. "Will you track the criminals, Mister Ryland? Undoubtedly the brigands have left the area, but it would reassure our clientele to know that a law officer was on the case already."

"What about Mister Hussey here? He already knows the area."

Both Parker and Hussey were adamant in their negative response. "Constable's job is to keep the peace in town, not run around the countryside," Hussey said. "It was Wells, Fargo took the biggest loss. I figure that makes it your job to do the tailin'." Parker nodded his agreement.

Unfortunately, I had to concur with their assessment. "Was anyone hurt?"

"After what happened to Bledsoe—" Hussey asserted.

"And to you," Parker added, pointing to my head.

"Nobody wanted to be a hero," Hussey concluded.

"Can somebody fix me a canteen and some food?" I said. "I'll head out while it's still light."

"Already done," Parker declared, passing me a leather knapsack.

"Then there's just one more thing. Was any particular notice taken of the voice of any one of the robbers?"

"Yes," Hussey agreed. "Now that you mention it. The driver and two of the passengers commented on how the leader of the thieves had a kind of gravelly note to his words, even though he otherwise sounded young."

"Thanks," I said. "Now, how about directions to the holdup site?"

The road beyond Georgetown was even more deserted than the lower stretch had been. Volcanoville was a lonely mining camp practically perched on the edge of the gorge of the middle fork of the American River. The stage down from there only ran twice each week.

Since I was still mounted on Ophelia it was fortunate that I did not have to traverse all seventeen miles of rutted gravel. Constable Hussey told me that the site of the ambush would be easy to locate because of the freshly cut trees beside the road.

I asked Juan and Armando to accompany me, but this was vetoed by Mr. Parker, their employer. He said they had wasted enough time and could not be spared for more pointless foolishness.

Truth to tell, I was getting a bit irked that no one seemed to think my efforts would amount to anything.

I freely admitted that I was a newcomer to the West, and unfamiliar with many of its peculiarities. Even so, being a novice did not mean I was completely without the capacity to learn and learn quickly. I determined to be businesslike and professional, whether or not immediate results were obtained.

It was late afternoon that I arrived at a short horse-shoe bend in the trail in the shadow of Bald Mountain. Even if I had not heard of the masks and slickers, I could have figured out that this job was pulled by the same bunch as waylaid my coach. Just at the place where the road dipped and started to climb Hotchkiss Hill, a pair of oaks had been felled. The ropes with which they were finally dragged aside were still looped around the branches.

A chipmunk ran out on one of the tree trunks and chattered at me. Tying Ophelia to a limb, I dismounted to study the ground.

The wheel marks of the coach were plain in the red dirt, as were several sets of boot prints. These so crossed and recrossed each other that they told me nothing.

Walking a spiralling path, I looped around and around the holdup scene, moving a little farther out from the center on each pass. I found where two robbers had taken cover in some rocks above the road, two had hidden in a clump of elderberries, and two more had been below the lip of the ravine behind where the coach halted. One more brigand to do the talking and collect from the passengers and the total was seven, just like before. It was looking brighter and brighter for Tom Baker. I resolved to finish up quickly and then hurry back to Coloma with the report that might free him, or at least keep him from a date with Judge Lynch.

About a quarter mile east of the horseshoe curve, I came upon the spot where the highwaymen had tied their mounts. The outbound trail was also plain, since the seven horses broke quite a swath through the yarrow weeds. I retrieved Ophelia and we set off to follow.

It was unlikely that such an accomplished band would make the mistake of keeping together for long, nor did they. About a mile up the dry wash, the trail climbed out of the canyon onto a tableland that looked back over the robbery site. Here the group divided as I guessed. Two riders went east, two south, and two north toward the river.

The lone single rider who remained committed himself to a westerly path. It was this track that I elected to pursue. There were two motives for my choice: my own destination in aid of the falsely accused Baker lay in the same direction. Second, the tracks of the solitary traveller showed deeper hoofprints than the other mounts. It could mean nothing more than that it was a heavier man. But it could also portend that they had not divvied the loot. I was banking that if one single outlaw was trusted with the booty, it must be the gravel-throated leader. Such was my reasoning, anyway.

I do not say that I had a particular score to settle with that man, nor was revenge my conscious motivation. It did seem to me that overtaking the bandit chief would be the best thing I could do.

———◆———

The tracks of the bandit's horse were plain enough, all the way down the banks of the westering stream I later learned was called Canyon Creek. The man I was following seemed to have no fear of pursuit, for the hoofprints showed that beyond breaking into an occasional trot, there was no haste to his travel.

As I rode I reflected on the events of the past few days. The first robbery had taken place away east, up that fork of the river. Jim Hume had set the posses out toward all compass points, but they had not cut the trail of the gang when it headed north. I even understood the reason for that error. Since Tom Baker, now sweating in the stone and steel cage in Coloma, had been captured north of the river, Hume believed that the other members of the gang had gone elsewhere, reasoning that they split up to confuse the pursuit.

Somehow the outlaws had discovered that the search was concentrating everywhere but where they actually were. That news emboldened them to accomplish the second holdup such a short time after the first.

It had been twelve hours since the robbery of the Georgetown stage, which meant that unless the bandits had gone to ground already, they undoubtedly had crossed streams to cover their trails. Certainly they had a preplanned rendezvous at which they would meet, settle up, and plan their next job.

Since Hume and company were still off south, it only made sense that the highwaymen would eventually go north. I was certain now that they would cross the middle fork of the American and disappear into the hills on the Nevada City side of the stream.

I had no illusions about being able to round them up myself. If I could just get an idea of where they were headed, it would be a start.

Ophelia and I rode all the bright summer evening and into the gloom that finally descended over the western Sierra. Twice I lost the trail where my quarry crossed patches of bare rock, but I picked up the trace again on the far side.

Once the outlaw doubled back on his own path, making me wonder if my conjecture was all wrong. The tracks looped around a small knoll, then cut abruptly to the south and up to the top of the hill.

I located the spot where he had rested the horse. He must have been studying his back trail, looking for signs of pursuit. The robber had taken a chaw from a plug of Raleigh Five Star tobacco; I know because he discarded the cloth pouch.

Little by little I was building a portrait of the man. Besides his rough voice and the fact that he chewed tobacco (not very exclusive traits at that), I had learned that he was brazen enough to rob two stages within a week no more than forty miles apart. He was confident enough in his ability to foil the chase that he made little effort to confuse his tracks, but still cautious enough to study his back trail. I guessed one more thing: he had either been able to sneak into town to gather intelligence about the activities of the posse, or else he had informants placed to carry him word.

The question now was this: What direction did I take? I could not keep the trace in the dark, and by tomorrow the trail would be cold. It would be better for me to turn back and head to Coloma to communicate my findings to Jim Hume when the lawman returned.

I was not confident enough of my own ability to take out across country for Coloma. I did judge that if I headed south I would strike the Coloma-Georgetown road. It was with this thought in mind that I wheeled Ophelia around.

It was at that moment that I saw the light. Low on the horizon it was, like an orange star just above the rim of the earth. I realized that I was seeing lamp or firelight, and that it was directly in line with the bearing taken by my quarry.

It was long odds that the bandit chief would stop while still so near the scene of the robbery, and yet I was minded to reconnoiter anyway. Someone might have seen the man I was seeking or be able to provide some clue.

Rolling hills spread down in the direction of the river, and each time Ophelia and I descended one we would lose sight of our goal. Each time we climbed another ridge the light would still beckon us on farther west.

Drawing rein on the brow of a low mound cluttered with scrubby oaks and buckeye, I studied my destination. The glow I had seen was coming from the upper window of a two-story log cabin. The building looked old but sturdy. The walls of the lower floor were solid, having no windows in them and only one small entry that I could see. It had the appearance of being as much fort as dwelling. It came to me that I might have stumbled directly upon the bandit hideout, here in the wilds above the river gorge, miles from any settlement.

What to do? I was alone. I had no weapon, and even if I had, no skill that would set me equal to practiced gunmen. Yet I could not leave without knowing something of the identity of the occupants of such an isolated spot.

My one concession to caution was to ride far around the building before approaching it. The last thing I wanted to communicate to the inhabitants was that I had come to their quarters directly along the trail from the holdup.

When I got to within a hundred yards I decided to provoke a response and await the result. I hollered, "Holloa, the cabin. I've lost my way. Can you direct me to the road to Coloma?"

"Clear off," a high-pitched voice whined. Whoever the speaker was, he could not be the outlaw captain. This relaxed me some, I confess.

"I just need some help," I returned, nudging Ophelia forward. "I won't bother you for long."

"I said, be off with ye," the voice repeated in what I reckoned to be a Scottish accent. "I'll nay be put upon again."

The word "again" barely had time to register when there was a snap and a roar and a jet of flame from the upper story. A stand of willows crackled and splintered with the passage of a load of buckshot, and Ophelia snorted and reared. I had been shot at twice in one day!

"Hold on!" I called. "I'm unarmed and lost. I just want to ask for directions. My name is Ryland and I'm an agent with Wells, Fargo."

"That's just what t'other feller said," the unseen sentry said. "Now away with ye!"

"What other fellow?"

"The one that coom along last night! Said there was a holdup and he needed some help. Said he was with Wells, Fargo. I undid ma latch to look down the muzzle of a forty-four. Took ma poke, he did! Near four hundred dollars in dust!"

"This bandit," I said, excitement rising in me. "Did he have a curious rough voice for a young man?"

"Aye," the Scotsman cautiously agreed. "What of it?"

"That's the man I've been tracking," I explained. "The real bandit chief. Can you tell me anything about his looks? Anything that might help me capture him?"

There was a pause of lengthy consideration, then the Scotsman said, "Ye'd best coom in. Just dismount where ye are and coom to the gate with hands up."

Fergus Macreedy was hopping mad . . . literally. The diminutive Scotsman, whose height came but a hand span above my middle, bounced from one foot to the other in wrath and indignation. "I tell ye," he said, flecks of spittle spinning free of his grizzled beard, "I tell ye, if I coom within gunshot of yon misbegotten wretch, I'll make such a sieve of him that . . . that . . ." Here he sputtered to a stop, unable to define the number of holes with which the robber would be ventilated. "There'll be more of air ta him than substance I tell ye," he concluded at last.

Recounting for me again the events of the preceding night, Macreedy explained how he was duped into letting a snake into his burrow. "Said a wee lad was hurt in the gunplay," he stormed. "I could nay refuse to help, could I? And as I unbarred the portal, he stuck the muzzle of his cursed great pistol up ma nostril. Said ta show him the gold or else."

By the time the tale was told I had added one more stroke to the portrait of the highwayman: apparently success made him insolently brazen. Without regard to the fact that a posse might be close behind, the blackguard did not hesitate to perform more wickedness. Ignoring the fact that the law would be grateful for a description of his face, the villain had confidently talked his way into the old hermit's stronghold and robbed him! This event came no more than a few hours after the stage holdup, during his getaway.

"Did he slip with a name of any in his gang?" I asked.

The question made Macreedy spew invective again. "Proud as sin," the Scotsman ranted. "Gave his own name."

Fascinated, I inquired, "And what was it?"

"When I told him he would swing for all his deviltry, he laughed in ma face! Thumped his chest and swore a blaspheming oath that none could touch Tom Baker or his gang!"

Tom Baker! Now there was a riddle to wrestle with! I had left Tom Baker securely incarcerated in Coloma, so it could not be the same man. Yet what an amazing conjunction of names.

"And his voice?" I asked. "Can you tell me about his voice?"

"Aye, that I kin," Macreedy agreed. "'Twas like a grist-mill inta which some prankster slipped a can of rocks."

Here was the confirmation that I had in fact been trailing the leader of the outlaw band. Further, it told me that the young man in the hoosegow was another step nearer freedom, despite his unfortunate name.

Macreedy carried on at some length about the bandit's voice without adding any new insight, then fell to fuming again about his violated sanctuary. "Thirty-eight year since I run away ta sea," he said. "Twenty-eight year since I jumped ship and escaped from the foul-smelling hulk of a hide trader off Spanish California.

Eighteen years gone since ma wife run off with ma trading partner and I coom ta these mountains ta live alone. Trapping at first and later gold . . . gold I had in plenty for ma needs, until last night! Rot Tom Baker's black heart and hide!"

"Mister Macreedy," I interrupted. "I will do all I can to recover your gold. But there is more you can do to help yourself. You are the only man who has seen the robber's face. Can you describe him?"

Reaching up with both hands, Macreedy pulled his wool bonnet down over his ears and dropped his chin toward his chest. In that attitude he sat for a long while, and then he said, "I should nay be so angry. Fury has like ta stole my wits and I canna think what ta say."

"Young or old?" I prompted.

"Youngish," he said. "But a man grown. Much of your own age, I should think."

"Tall? short?"

"Not a great sprout like yourself, but taller than me."

I reflected that to be taller than Mr. Macreedy indicted most of California. "Bearded?"

"Nay!" Macreedy stated with satisfaction. "Clean-shaven."

"Hair color? Eyes?"

Macreedy pondered again, then shook his head sadly. He pursed his lips at last and made a whooshing noise. "Ach, laddie, I kin no more than I said already."

The portrayal given was so general as to be almost useless. It fit thousands of miners and townsfolk, excluding only the Mexicans and the Chinese. It could even be fairly applied to the other Tom Baker back in Coloma.

"Will ye spend the night, Mister Ryland?" Macreedy asked. "'Tis the least I can do after nearly blowing your head from your shoulders."

"No," I said. "Thank you. If you can point the way to the Coloma road I'll be on my way."

At that moment we both heard the sound of hoofbeats approaching the lodge, and then a voice called out, "Holloa, the cabin. Can you give us a drink and show us the road?"

"Not again!" Macreedy snarled, starting up and snatching his shotgun from a rack made of elk antlers.

"Hold on," I said. "They could be harmless like me."

"Laddie," Macreedy said, waving me back with a swing of the gun's barrel. "I chose this spot for its peace and quiet. Dinna ye think it a bit queer ta have so many guests come calling? Innocent, be hanged! It gives me new doubts about ye!"

With that he motioned me to back up to the far wall.

Meanwhile the voice outside hollered again. "Did you hear me in there? I said, can you spare a drink?"

The voice sounded familiar, but who did I know to be riding in the wild at night? For that matter, how many folks in these parts did I know at all?

"I believe I'd rather not," Macreedy replied. "Just you ride on. I'm armed and I mean ta defend maself."

"What are you gabbling about?" the unseen caller asked. "We don't mean any harm. We've ridden far and only need a drink and directions."

"Directions, is it?" Macreedy fairly screamed. "Do ye think me daft?" And with that he thrust the scatter-gun's barrel out the window and blasted away. Outside on the hillside, men yelled, horses called in alarm, and pounding hoofbeats resounded as the party scattered. "And I've got another barrel ready for ye!" Macreedy warned. Then to me he added, "And do not ye be stir-ring neither."

"Stop that shooting," came the command from out-side. "I am Deputy Sheriff Hume and this is a posse in pursuit of stage robbers. I order you to throw down your gun and open the door."

"Aye, and I'm Saint Andrew," Macreedy replied. "And here is my order ta ye!"

At the instant he raised the shotgun to his shoulder, I flung myself across the room and slammed into the old man. The blunderbuss, jolted sideways, blasted up into the night sky. From outside came the shout, "Let him have it, men," and gunfire popped all around the cabin. Bullets thudded against the thick walls and several rounds came through the window to smack against the wall where I had lately been standing.

Macreedy and I rolled over and over on the floor. He kicked me in the shins, clawed at me with inch-long nails, and bit my nose. Finally I got uppermost, put my knees on his arms, and pinned his snapping jaws down by holding the gun stock across his neck.

"Jim!" I shouted. "Jim Hume. Stop shooting. It's me, Ryland."

"Ryland?" Hume yelled back. "What the Sam Hill did you shoot at us for?"

"It wasn't me," I called. "Just give me a minute and I'll open the door and explain." To Macreedy I said, "He's telling the truth, Mister Macreedy. I recognize his voice. Now just be easy while I let him in."

Macreedy sulked in a corner of his retreat like a wounded animal while I unbolted and unbarred the entry. I explained the situation to Hume and the three men who rode with him, including all that Macreedy had told me about the robber. "But how do you come to be here?" I asked. "I thought you were away south."

"So I was till midday," Hume said. "Then I got word about the second holdup so I rode cross-country, figuring that the outlaws would head north. I wanted to cut them off before they reached the river, or at least cut their trail along here."

"Well," I said with some satisfaction. "You did, but I beat you to it."

Finally convincing the Scotsman that we were not more reivers come to steal, I gave Macreedy back his shotgun, unloaded, of course.

Over a lean supper of jerked venison, hard biscuits, and the springwater, which was Macreedy's only beverage, Hume and I exchanged information. I told him all my conclusions about the robber captain, and we pondered together about the confusion of names.

I made a final promise to Macreedy that I would attempt to recover his gold if he would not shoot at me when I returned. Then I joined the posse and we set off northward.

Besides Macreedy's grudging directions to the river, Jim Hume had an uncanny ability to keep the trail even by moonlight, getting down from his horse on occasion to reconfirm his thoughts. Before daybreak the hoofprints crossed the middle fork of the American River, and that is when we lost the spoor.

We split into two groups and searched both directions and both banks, just in case the outlaw had doubled back, but no further trace could we find. At last Hume agreed that I should return to Coloma to convey the good news to the imprisoned Tom Baker. Hume and his men would continue the search for another day.

At the conclusion of two and a half days in the saddle, I possessed three unsolved robberies (counting Macreedy's gold), a horse old enough to have welcomed explorer Jedidiah Smith to California in the 1820s, too many saddle sores to count, and an overwhelming sense of futility. Worst of all, I had lost the little meat that had been added to my bones by the cooking of Mrs. Nichols, Ling, and Eliza.

CHAPTER 7

It was hot the afternoon of my return to Coloma. The early autumn air was thick with the scent of tarweed and dust. The shouts of children playing in the schoolyard echoed against the hills across the river. The reins were slack as Ophelia plodded toward the barn behind the Wells, Fargo office. The old mare was ready for a flake of hay and a long, cool drink of water from her own trough.

The yeasty, cool scent of fermenting brew turned my weary head as we passed the brewery. My mouth was watering and I pictured myself stretching out on the settee of my office for a long nap.

Then the raucous shouts of Eliza's pupils drew my mind back from my desire for comfort. The sheaf of notes and depositions in my saddlebag contained momentous news, did it not? I had promised Eliza to give her the word the moment I returned, had I not? And what about poor Tom Baker, rotting in the jail? I had enough new evidence to open wide the door to his cell.

I reined Ophelia to a halt fifty yards from the barn. She fought me a moment, stretched her neck against the bit, then swung her jug head around to nip the toe of my boot.

"Sorry, old girl," I said. "Better for you to wait than Eliza." Reluctant and balky, Ophelia carried me to Coloma School.

Eliza stood, hands on hips, glowering down at two adolescent boys who were partners in some play-yard crime. One was a brown-complected teen; his cohort a lighter-hued sprout.

One quick glance at the Bledsoe alphabet pack told me that the transgression had somehow involved them. Adam Bledsoe, lip swollen and nose bleeding, stood defiantly glaring out from the circle of Bette, Chloe, Danette, and little Eve. Adam's four sisters looked as though they, too, were ready to go to warring. The other children in the school yard clustered beneath the huge oak tree and whispered behind their hands.

I had come at an awkward time. As if reading my longing to ride elsewhere, Ophelia rebelled. In spite of my attempt to rein her around, she planted her four hooves in the road, waited a moment, then lunged forward until her chest touched the hitching rail. She had come far enough with me on her back and she would go no farther.

I dismounted the stubborn animal as if this were what I intended to do all along. The Mexican lad and his companion glanced my way. Eliza's gaze followed theirs.

Spotting me, her already firm expression turned to stone. Had I done something wrong? Beneath that withering look I felt like a guilty schoolboy once again.

I waved in a clumsy, embarrassed fashion, patted Ophelia on the neck, and called, "Don't mind me. You go right ahead with what you're doing."

"You're back, are you? Wait there."

As I look back on the greeting, it beats me why I was so enraptured with Eliza Richardson. She ordered me around like one of her students, scolded me in the same tone of voice as my mother had used, and let me know in a thousand little ways that she thought I was a green-horn and an Eastern-bred fool who had no business being west of the Rockies.

I countered, "I've got business down at the jail."

"Not anymore you don't," she snapped. "I'll have a word with you as soon as I sort this out." She turned her back on me and directed the spectator students back into the schoolhouse. The Mexican youth and his compatriot were led by their ears to separate tree stumps, plopped down, and ordered not to budge. The Bledsoe children crammed their furious faces into the window frames and stared at me as if I were the cause of all their problems.

It was enough. Remounting Ophelia, I nudged her, tugged the reins, gave her a swift kick in the ribs. She would not budge. I decided that Eliza had an amazing power of intimidation.

So there I sat; the hot sun beating on my dusty back; my horse snoozing in disregard of my authority.

Educational matters well in hand at last, Eliza whirled and strode toward me.

I tried to smile. Tipping my hat in a most friendly fashion, I explained briefly about the second robbery and the fact that the leader of that gang had possessed a raspy voice. Tom Baker was exonerated, despite his grating speech.

She brushed my news aside. "Hang it all! Tom Baker flew the coop two nights ago."

"He what?"

"Broke out. He's gone. Vamoosed before he got hung."

"But . . . but . . . but . . ." I stammered in disbelief. My fuddled brain filled with a thousand questions. I managed to spit out, "How?"

"Ask Ollie. I have no time for this. You've broken your word and the result is chaos and anarchy in my classroom."

This accusation was a double blow. "But I wasn't even here," I protested. Flies buzzed around Ophelia's head. I wondered if the old mare had died beneath me and been seized with rigor mortis. There was no running away from the anger in Miss Eliza's voice.

She put her hand on the horse's neck and glared up at me. "No, you were not here. But you promised that Wells, Fargo would not leave the Bledsoe family destitute, and you have forsaken that promise."

"I have not, Miss Eliza!"

"The news came yesterday that Wells, Fargo and Company will not pay one penny toward the welfare of this family. Five children and one on the way . . ."

"Another one!" I cried. So there was to be a letter F added to the flock of little ducks.

"Yes, yes, yes." Eliza lowered her voice. "Little Frank or Francine to feed! And contrary to your solemn oath, the baby is coming into a hard and cruel world where company agents go back on their promises and fatherless children are regarded without compassion or mercy."

"But why not?"

Eliza said through gritted teeth, "Because Nick Bledsoe was employed by the Pioneer Stage and not by your precious express company!"

I was without defense. I had made an oath. Wells, Fargo would not honor it. "Was this what the boys were fighting about?"

She tossed her head. "Indeed. Those two," she indicated the boys on the stumps, "called the Bledsoe children little beggars. Among other things. The word is out all right. Half the town thinks you ought to be tarred and feathered and run out of town on a rail."

I winced at the sentiment, wondering what the other half thought was appropriate punishment. I shuddered in spite of the heat, and then got hold of my wits. "Long as I work for Wells, Fargo, my word is the company's word. My word is my bond. It will be as I said on that first day. It may take time, but you shall see."

This sudden bravado on my part seemed to startle Eliza. She almost smiled. "Well, then. Well, well. Splendid."

"Now," I said importantly. "I have business at the jail." My voice cracked as I broached the next subject. "May I call on you, Miss Eliza?"

A slow smile. Did the question amuse her? Or was she pleased? "You may." With that, she slapped Ophelia on the rump and said, "Get to the barn, old girl."

Ophelia jerked her head up, spun on her heels, and trotted smartly back down the road to the barn.

Words can hardly express the spinning of my brain over this unexpected turn of events. If the Tom Baker captured by the posse was not still in the Coloma lockup, then could he be the same man seen by Macreedy? I had already noted the resemblance of descriptions and voices. I shook my head with more vigor than Ophelia showed chasing flies.

I told myself to slow down and think straight. The Georgetown stage had been robbed two nights before, when the Tom Baker I knew was still in jail. So it could not be the same man, could it?

This speculation was leading nowhere. I was hopeful that Ollie could shed some light on what had happened. Riding directly to the prison, I left Ophelia to graze the bunchgrass in the field while I strode toward the open door of the stockade. "Ollie," I called. "Where are you?"

There was no reply. A quick glance inside showed no Ollie Turnipseed. Vexed, I threw Ollie's carpetbag off the stool and onto the floor. I slammed open the grate of the iron cell and ducked my head to plunge inside. I tipped over the cot and shook out the blankets, as if I might find Tom Baker or perhaps Ollie hiding beneath. When I had vented my spleen, it came to me that with the prisoner gone, what reason was there for Ollie to remain at the jail? He was probably in one of the cafes or saloons.

Chagrined at my lack of control, I set the cot back upright and bent over to retrieve the blanket. It was while I was stooped low that something caught my eye. In the adjoining cell, on the floor, back in the farthest, darkest corner was a small, pale-colored object, like a torn piece of clothing.

More out of curiosity than expectation, I went into the second chamber and picked up the article. It was a sack of Raleigh Five Star chewing tobacco, empty of its original contents, but with something inside that rustled. I undid the string and took out a scrap of paper. Squinting in the dim interior, I could see that there was something written on the fragment, but I could not make it out till I went back outside.

On a bit of waxed butcher paper were the words, "Don't lose hop, Tom. Yew will be out soon," spelled exactly as I have recorded them.

So Tom Baker had an accomplice in aid of his escape. Well, that only made good sense. But who? How had the note arrive? While I pondered all these things, who should wander into view but Ollie Turnipseed himself.

At first sight my hand shot up to the side of my head. The reason for this strange reaction was simple: on the side of Ollie's noggin was a lump of cotton wool bound in place with yards of bandages, much like the one that had graced my own. A picture jumped to my head of two lodge fellows of a strange and mystic order, identified by lumpy headgear. He looked so odd that it was hard not to laugh. Just two things stopped me: the woebegone expression on his normally cheerful face and the realization that if he looked eccentric, then so had I.

"Ollie," I said, anger all put aside. "What happened?"

"Wish you could tell me," he replied. "Do you think they'll fire me?" he asked. "Lost a shipment from the coach, then lost the prisoner, too. Will they give me the shove, Jack?"

"Take it easy," I said gently, leading him toward the stool and making him sit down. "Tell me what you can."

"Two nights ago," he began. "I settled down to guarding for the night. Things was mostly quiet."

"Hold it right there," I instructed. "Are you telling me that Baker escaped day before yesterday? Not last night?"

"Ain't that what I just started to tell you?" he said peevishly, holding his head in one hand and rocking sideways. "Supper come from the Sierra Nevada about seven. Miss Eliza sent me and the prisoner some apple pie 'long about nine. You come over about ten. Then, close to eleven, Judge Magee come by. Said he wanted to warn me 'bout some rough talk goin' on at the saloon."

"What kind of rough talk?"

"More jawin' 'bout lynchin' Baker for killin' Nick. Well, I weren't too worried about that. Said I'd lock myself in again and send for the preacher."

"And then?"

"Sometime near twelve, Judge Magee sent Pedro, that's the barkeep, over with a jug of coffee. Said to keep alert, 'cause the noisy ones was gettin' even louder." The shotgun messenger paused and raised bloodshot and swollen eyes to look me in the face. "Next thing I knowed, it was morning, I was thumped on the head, and the prisoner was gone."

I was stunned as much as the guard. "You're sure you locked the door back?"

Ollie looked even sadder. "I can't remember. I think so. Anyway, I tried to let you know first thing, but you'd already rid out for Georgetown. Judge Magee pert near flayed me alive. He got a bunch of his men together to comb the hills, but they didn't find nothing yet."

So there it was. Ollie had fallen asleep. Either he had forgotten to lock the entry or someone had a duplicate key. They had taken the guard unawares, knocked him senseless to keep him out of the way and freed Baker.

The breakout occurred about midnight. It took four hours or so to ride to where the holdup of the Georgetown stage took place; perfect timing for a robbery that happened a couple hours before dawn. It could have been Tom Baker who robbed the coach and Macreedy . . . then the absurdity of my thoughts hit me like a thunderbolt: it *was* Tom Baker. There were not two men with the same name. There was one murderous, thieving wretch, and I had been afraid for his life!

It was nearly suppertime when I left Ollie at the jail, but I was not hungry. Two matters troubled me deeply: according to Eliza, Wells, Fargo had betrayed the destitute family of Nick Bledsoe. It was no good me trying to explain the correctness of the doctrine that Nick had worked for the Pioneer Stage Company and not for the express company and that the Pioneer ownership was responsible; that would only sound to her like an excuse. The burden of the company failure rested squarely upon my shoulders.

What could I do to assist the widow and those children? I briefly imagined myself capturing the entire gang and collecting a reward to turn over to Mrs. Bledsoe. A single glance at my reflection in the window of Bell's Store convinced me that such a thought was absolute foolishness. The image of Ichabod Crane reared up to shame me.

To top off my desolation, Tom Baker, whom I had believed to be innocent, proved his guilt by bolting from the jail in the middle of the night. He had gone on to join his gang and rob the Georgetown stage. I was a fool. The company would, no doubt, learn of my incompetence and ship me back to Princeton in the boot of a Concord stagecoach.

With these unhappy thoughts drumming in my head, I returned Ophelia to her stall. Mr. Creedmore, fully dressed in his undertaker's finery, greeted me at the barn door.

"Well now, if it ain't Agent Ryland, returned from the wars. Guess you heard the news about Tom Baker. A clean break it was," he said cheerfully. "Shoulda give the preacher time to deal with Baker's soul and then hung that rascal when we had the chance."

I ignored the gibe. "I've not got all the details."

"Bad news can wait, as we say in my business." The undertaker tugged at his collar. "Sooner or later it arrives."

"You're dressed to greet bad news," I remarked, slipping saddle and bridle from Ophelia, who wandered back to her stall without my assistance.

Creedmore stared at his reflection in a smoky mirror tacked up to a horse stall. He straightened his black tie and waistcoat and I swear he smiled at himself. "Got a call to make over in Chinatown. There's an old vacarro married himself a Chinese woman. Doc says he'll die soon of the consumption and he's scared to death his wife's relatives will cremate him as the Celestials sometimes do. He's a Catholic and don't fancy taking the ashes to ashes part of the ceremony too literal. Nothing like a fine pine coffin and a team of black horses to comfort a dying man." He tipped his stovepipe hat to me, turned to leave, and then thought better of it. His smile faded as he lectured me one last time. "You and that bonehead preacher made a big mistake in this Tom Baker affair. I for one will look forward to burying the man who murdered good old Nick."

How could I reply? "In due time and the course of law you will hopefully enjoy that privilege."

It crossed my mind to saddle up Ophelia and ride out in search of Tom Baker. After standing up for him, getting my nose rubbed in the dirt to keep him from getting lynched, and generally being abused by townspeople who believed him guilty of murder, I was ready to track him, seize him, and even hang him myself.

It was that last thought that helped me recover my balance. Something Eliza said the night of the almost lynching came back to me: "If he runs, no one will ever believe he's innocent," or words to that effect. Was I being guilty of jumping to that same conclusion now, along with everyone else in Coloma?

What if he had not escaped, but instead had been dragged out of his cell to face a vigilante court and sudden justice at the end of a rope? Just because Pastor

Pierce had cooled out the mob once did not mean they would stay quiet; I had Ollie's own report on that score.

I wanted to question Judge Magee. He could give me some leads as to who was doing the rough talking that he had warned Ollie about. But when I got to the Metropolitan Saloon, Pedro, the bartender, told me that Magee had ridden over to Placerville and would be gone all day.

My one source gone and nobody much else even speaking to me, I decided there was only one course of action left. If Baker had not escaped but had been forcibly removed from the cell, then the odds were great that he was already dead and buried in a canyon not far from Coloma.

So I also embarked on a pursuit, but with an important difference: instead of hunting a fugitive, I was in search of a corpse. I went on foot, expecting that if I was correct, Baker's abductors would not have taken him far. They would have covered the evidence of their deed in some brush-and-rubble-choked gully where a horse and rider could not penetrate.

Back of Coloma, to the west, there are several canyons to which that description applied. The hill at the very edge of town reared up sharply and its slope was smothered with locust trees, oaks, elderberry brambles, and buckeye tangles. I picked the likeliest dry wash and started searching.

I carried the shotgun suggested by Eliza. I laughed at myself because on the previous occasions when there might have been gunplay, I had not remembered the weapon. This time, if my hunch proved out, there was no danger. Still, best to go prepared.

Hours passed. I sweated more pounds off my lean frame, but I swear the scattergun gained the weight and about fifty pounds more besides. I made a sling of my belt and carried the twelve gauge over my shoulder. In that span of afternoon, I discovered thorns and burrs beyond counting, a nest of hornets, and a skunk whose right to possess a hollow tree trunk I did not stop to dispute. I was grateful when the sun finally dropped below the rim of the hill, because I was parched.

When I reached the head of the canyon without any result, I sat down on a rock to rest and looked back over the grade I had climbed. There was no indication that anyone had come up that way in a hundred years; neither boot nor hoofprint, and certainly no sign of a body. If Tom Baker was dead and buried, then he was just going to have to stay that way.

I sat long enough to watch the evening shadows lengthen and the interlaced fingers of the buckeye limbs become dark tunnels. It was that change of the light that attracted my attention to a low mound just below a rocky outcropping. I had not seen it before in the bright sunshine, but in silhouette it stood out. The embankment was not a natural feature, of that much I was certain, and it was the right size and shape to be the heap of dirt and brush above a hastily dug grave. Leaves and weeds had been strewn over the place to conceal it, and the camouflage had almost been successful.

The sense of triumph at having spotted the hidden location was quickly tempered by the recollection of what it was I had discovered. Almost without thinking, I unslung the shotgun and checked to see that the caps were in place.

As I approached the spot, I stopped and turned completely around, surveying the canyon and the hillsides and the boulders. I paid particular attention to the dark areas under the rims of the ledges and those shadows formed by overhanging boughs.

I told myself that I was studying the surroundings for signs; clues that might lead me to Tom Baker's murderers. The truth? I was plain nerved up. If a child had as much as said "boo" I would have shucked my skin on the spot.

From a dozen yards away, the air was tainted with the coppery, metallic smell of death. There could be no mistake: Baker had been slaughtered and buried, and the perpetrators thought to go free by making it look like a jailbreak.

By coming out without Ophelia I had no means to pack the body back to Coloma. In fact, I did not even have a tarp in which to wrap it.

At least I could tumble some more rocks down over the grave to protect it from scavenging animals until I could guide others back. I set to work, knocking chunks of quartz free from the cliff above and heaping them on the brush.

The darkness was closing in and I wanted to be done and away. A piece of brush sticking up in the center of the mound interfered with my rock pile and I stooped to pull it free. What a terrible hurry Baker's murderers had been in, to discard the body in such a shallow, uncaring way.

Holding my breath against the stench, I wrestled with the stubborn limb. The hair on my neck stood up because I seemed to be grappling with the corpse!

Then I wrenched the mesquite branch free, and uncovered . . . a deer carcass. The head was missing and the remains had been gnawed, but the mound clearly contained what was left of a buck and not Tom Baker at all.

Before I even had time to cuss myself as seven kinds of a fool, the depths of the canyon erupted in a scream! My hair stood straight up, this time clear from the back of my neck to the crown of my head. It was like a woman's shriek, but full of rage. When the outcry ended in a snarl, I knew it was not from a human throat.

I thumbed back both hammers of the shotgun. The problem was, I did not even know for certain from which direction the screech had come. I was trying to look every way at once, and so could not watch my feet. The second time I stubbed my toe on some unnoted stone, I cautiously let the hammers down before I could fall and blow my own head off.

I stayed high up on the hillside; there was no way I was going down into the brush and dark of the arroyo. Also, I forced myself to walk slowly and deliberately, instead of giving in to my natural inclination.

Even so, my return to Coloma was much quicker than the outbound journey had been. Great was my relief when I topped the last hill above the little valley and looked out on the lights of the small community.

I came back a much different route from the one I had taken earlier. In the dark I was not certain of the road, but figured that if I went straight down the slope I would arrive back on Main Street.

So when I came to a split-rail fence, I did not try to go around, but stepped over and continued on. About six paces into the field, my ankle caught on a trip wire. A whole string of cans rattled and clattered and a match flame flared in the window of a cabin that I had not even noticed in the darkness.

The cabin door was flung open with a crash and a man yelled, "Keep away from them pumpkins, you thievin' varmints!" This order was followed by an explosion as a shotgun blast deafened me.

I threw myself to the ground. "Don't shoot!" I yelled back. "I don't even want your pumpkins!"

"Well, come on out of there, then!" the guardian of the pumpkin patch commanded.

Shot at three times now, and all by mistake! Whatever I had read back in college about the wild and wooly West did not carry a patch on the reality!

Once I was back across the fence, the man wielding the shotgun asked, "What in thunder were you doin' there?"

"Lost my way," I explained. "Sorry for the disturbance. I'm just trying to get back to town."

"Well," he said slowly, "no harm done. Come on in. Coffee's still hot." By the slurring of his speech, I would have guessed his drink to be stouter than coffee.

Having joined the growing number of folks who took potshots at Jack Ryland, the owner of the cabin and the pumpkin field introduced himself as James Marshall. "And you're the Wells, Fargo fella, right?"

I reluctantly admitted to his assertion, expecting more criticism for my role in letting Tom Baker escape. I was wrong.

"Heard some of what happened when the mob from the Metropolitan got all liquored up," he said. "A bad business. It took courage for you to stand up to 'em like you done. I wouldn't want to see a lynching here in Coloma."

"Have you lived here long?" I asked.

Marshall gave me an odd, sideways look. "You could say so," he agreed. He had a lined and weather-beaten face, although he talked like a man in his mid-thirties. His gray eyes had several lifetimes of experience in them.

"And you raise pumpkins?" I looked around the walls of the cabin. Picks and shovels stood in one corner, beside a stack of gold pans. Another corner held rakes and spades. The rafters were hung with saws, planes, and drawknives. There seemed to be tools enough for a half dozen workmen.

Marshall followed my gaze around his living quarters with red-rimmed eyes, then favored me with another sidelong glance. "Got me an orchard, too . . . apples and so on. I prospect a little, and do a bit of woodwork when it's called for." Marshall shrugged off the discussion about himself by posing me a question. "Say, you made any progress on the stage robberies, or recapturing Baker?"

I told him about my concern that Baker had been lynched after all and my search of the canyons. "Makes sense," he agreed. "Someone stole a blanket off my clothesline the same night Baker disappeared. Wouldn't be surprised if he was buried in it."

Hesitating before coming to the end of the tale, I judged that Marshall was more friend than foe and plunged ahead. I told him about finding the deer's remains and then about the uncanny scream.

Marshall nodded, then said, "Mountain lion. Cougar'll rake brush over top of a kill if they can't carry it all back to their den at once . . . come back for it later. Scream you heard was prob'ly the same cat returning. Musta caught your smell on the breeze and thought you were stealin' his prey."

The explanation made me shudder all over again. I thanked him for the coffee and rose to leave.

"Do me a favor," he said at the door. "Folks who know me don't spread my name around to strangers. I'd appreciate it if you'd be mindful of that, too."

I agreed to the strange request, then tramped on back to town. On the way to my office, I stopped at the jail to see how Ollie was faring.

While there I mentioned the pumpkin man and his odd entreaty. "Sort of a hermit, is he?" I asked.

"Don't you know who that is?" Ollie said with wonder.

"He said his name was Marshall. Was he lying?"

Ollie roared. "That's the James Marshall . . . the one who started it all."

"You mean . . ."

"That's right! Not a half mile from where we're standin', James Marshall spotted the nugget in the tail-race of Cap'n Sutter's sawmill . . . begun the gold rush!"

"But that little cabin, and his garden?"

Shaking his head, Ollie explained, "James Marshall never made but beans and bacon money out of gold dust. He was always crowded out by other folks with more muscle or more guns. But that don't mean they left him alone . . . that's why he's a mite touchy about strangers. But don't take it exactly the way he said it."

"How so?"

"Since he discovered the first strike, word got around that he had a kind of magic touch. You know, a nose for gold. If he stopped to look over a prospect, a dozen characters would shove right on in next to him.

Followed him from camp to camp. Followed from one river to another. He got followed when he went to the necessary. Made him drink more'n was good for him . . . still does. Drink makes him forget that he don't like strangers. Drink makes him talk too much . . . talkin' makes him thirsty, so he drinks more, see? Gets so bad sometimes, he has to up and leave town."

CHAPTER 8

I retreated to the gloom of the Wells, Fargo office and stretched my aching bones on the cot. Soon I fell fast asleep.

However, my troubled dreams did not hold a candle to the drama that was about to unfold. It concerned the life of Eliza Richardson and the Emmanuel Church.

The church building was shared by the congregations of both Methodist and Episcopal denominations. This was an amiable arrangement for both creeds. The clerics rotated services in the surrounding hills, as they rode circuits of a hundred miles and more. On alternate Sundays Pastor Pierce took the pulpit while the Methodist preacher was out at a gold camp and vice versa. Likewise, members of each assemblage alternated weeks to clean the building.

When Pierce departed for a mining camp high in the Sierra, Eliza Richardson volunteered to spruce up the sanctuary for the incoming Methodists.

The moon rose over the valley just as Eliza and Doc Richardson finished their evening meal. Chin Lee and

Ling cleared the dishes and then announced that Ling's sister was about to deliver her seventh child and that word had come to summon Doc Richardson to the birth. The labor had grown difficult and there was concern for mother and child. In addition to this, Chin Lee and Ling begged to be excused from further household duties. Both wished to be on hand for the event.

Doc Richardson remarked, "Ling, Miss Eliza expected your help in tidying up the church this evening."

One look at Ling's crestfallen expression and Eliza dismissed the notion with a wave of her hand. "Go on, Ling. Chin Lee, leave the dishes. There's nothing so hard about mopping the floor of the church and straightening the hymnals."

And so it was that lantern, mop, and bucket in hand, Eliza set out to the church alone. She did not suspect what awaited her within those quiet walls.

The autumn night brought a chill with it. Eliza cleaned the grate of the potbellied stove in the center of the church, in preparation for the advancing season. She loaded it with wood but did not light the fire. The single lantern cast long shadows against the walls and a breeze outside stirred willow branches that tapped against the windowpanes as she worked. She felt no particular threat as she worked. She was preoccupied with the tragedy of the Bledsoe family and focused her mind on practical requests on their behalf, which she presented to the Almighty.

The hymnals distributed and dead altar flowers discarded, she began to mop the floor. Halfway finished with her task, she suddenly had the feeling that she was not alone.

The ceiling above her groaned as though someone were moving in the attic. She paused, leaned against her swab-brush and looked up. She would not have admitted to being frightened, but a chill coursed through her. Staring at the shadowed ceiling she waited for another footstep. There was only silence and the wind outside. Dismissing the notion that someone was in the crawl space above the ceiling, she returned to her task. Determined to overcome any twinge of nervousness, she began to sing a hymn. "Amazing grace, how sweet the sound, that saved a wretch like me . . ."

Moments passed and then the creak of the boards interrupted her. *Could it be the wind?* she wondered. Her question was answered when a fine shower of dust rained down onto the newly washed floor.

Eliza blinked at the film on the wet planks. She told herself that some schoolboy had climbed up the bell tower, entered the attic, and was out to terrify her as a prank. No doubt, unless she took the matter in hand, word would be all over the school yard next Monday that Miss Richardson was nothing but a yellow-bellied coward who believed in ghosts! Classroom discipline would be destroyed.

Her spine stiffened with resolve. She leaned her mop against the wall and, humming cheerfully now, she made her way to the belfry. Hiking her skirts, the dauntless Miss Eliza grabbed the lantern and climbed straight up the ladder.

It pleased her to imagine schoolboys crouching in terror at her approach. She would snatch them up by their ears, parade them home in humiliation to their parents, and have the last laugh! It was a pleasant vision, but it was not to be.

The rustle in the attic turned to a stumble and then a crash as the culprit fell in the darkness. "Stay where you are," Eliza called out. "You're caught and there's no getting out of here!"

Silence. Eliza stepped onto the landing where the bell hung. As she opened the door into the attic, she was grinning, certain of her victory. Holding the light high she crossed into the loft and peered around the rafters. Seeing no one, she cocked her head curiously to one side. She breathed in deeply, inhaling the sour smell of a man's sweat. The chill of her own fear returned.

"Who's here?" she cried, lurching back abruptly with the notion of fleeing down the ladder and fetching help.

In that instant a strong hand closed around her wrist. A man whispered harshly in her ear. "Do not move, Mizz Richardson."

She recognized the voice of Tom Baker. "Baker!" she cried as he pulled her against him and clamped his hand over her mouth.

"Don't struggle and I will not hurt you."

Eliza swung the lantern upward against his arm,

searing his flesh and causing him to give a muffled cry. He wrested the lamp from her and clutched her tighter, his forearm locked beneath her chin in a stranglehold.

Kicking him, Eliza fought until his desperate grip completely cut off her wind. Within moments she blacked out.

She did not know how long she lay unconscious. The sense of a soft breeze against her face awakened her. Her eyelids fluttered.

A man's worried voice soothed, "Mizz Richardson. Oh, Mizz Richardson. Didn't mean to knock you insensible, ma'am. I was afeard you was gonna scream, is all."

Eliza focused on Tom Baker, who was fanning her briskly with an open book. Clutching her throat, she regained her senses and her outrage. Sitting bolt upright she struck Baker in the face.

"You! Villain! Brigand!"

Stunned by the blow, he dropped the book and rocked back on his haunches. "I'm all them things. Indeed I am." He rubbed his cheek. "You pack a wallop, ma'am. And I ain't gonna say I don't deserve it, neither. If it's any comfort, I weren't out to do you no harm . . . just quiet you down some."

She groped for the rafters and clambered unsteadily to her feet. "It is no comfort. You're a desperado and an outlaw murderer . . ."

"But I ain't! I swear it, ma'am! I just found that there horse. I didn't do that stage driver nor nobody no harm."

"You may tell that to the judge and jury. You may tell that to the ten thousand who will come to see you hanged."

At her words, Baker came to his knees, clasped his hands together, and began to weep. "But you gotta believe me! You and that preacher saved my neck from the noose."

"And how did you repay us? By breaking out of jail and robbing yet another stage!"

Now Baker's face turned ashen. "Another . . ."

"Don't play me for a fool, Mister Baker. It's all over the county that your gang robbed the Georgetown stage and you were at the head of their villainy!"

"But I ain't been nowhere but here since them fellers turned me out of the stockade. I come right here lookin' for the padre, but he had up and gone. I ain't been no place else but here, a'grievin' and a'prayin' for my lost soul!"

"And well you should."

He held up the book with which he had fanned her. Eliza saw at once that it was a Bible. "I cain't read the words," he sobbed. "I know I'm bound to die, for I been framed up with this here robbery. They're gonna hang an innocent man. Leastwise I'm innocent of murder, though I got sin enough on my head that God Almighty gonna pitch me into the fiery lake. Oh, Mizz Richardson! I got no comfort for my damned soul and I cain't read these here words in the Good Book."

A hundred questions filled Eliza's mind. If Tom Baker had led a gang of robbers to attack the Georgetown stage, what was he doing back in Coloma? In the attic of the Emmanuel Church?

She asked, "Who turned you loose?"

Wiping his eyes with the back of his filthy hand he replied, "I don't know who, ma'am. It was all dark, see? First off I thought they had come to finish me. Then somebody hit the guard and told me to get a'goin'. I didn't wait to ask no more questions."

Eliza cast her gaze around the cramped space. In the corner was a blanket. Eliza recognized it as the quilt that James Marshall had reported stolen off his clothesline the morning after the jailbreak.

"Where'd you get that?" she demanded.

"I sort of . . . borrowed it. I lit a shuck through some garden in the dark the night I broke out and ran smack into a clothesline. I'll give it back though."

She eyed a bucket half filled with water. "And the bucket?"

"I got powerful thirsty, ma'am. So yesterday night I sneaked down and took it from the church well."

She frowned, remembering that when she had stopped by two days ago to mop the floor there had been no bucket with which to draw water. That fact had turned her back from doing the cleaning before tonight. It came to her in a flash that if Tom Baker was here to steal the water bucket and the blanket then he could not have ridden to Georgetown to pull another stage heist.

She asked the pitiful creature who knelt before her, "When did you eat last?"

"I reckon it was before I run away."

"Three days?"

"Yes'm, I reckon that long. I cain't rightly recollect how long."

"You must be hungry."

"Yes'm." He glanced down at the Bible in his hands. "But if they're a'gonna catch me and hang me, I'm a sight more in need of someone who can read me this here book. I'm mostly too scared to eat. My belly don't matter no more. It's my soul that's a'hungerin'. You can read to me a spell before you hand me over, cain't you, ma'am?"

Eliza took the Bible from the young man's hands. "Where shall I begin?"

He shook his head. "I ain't saved. Ain't been baptized, neither. You think they'll let me get baptized before they stretch my neck, ma'am?"

Eliza could not speak for a moment as she thumbed through the pages. Her eyes locked on the first epistle of Saint John. Clearing her throat she began to read. "If we confess our sins, He is faithful and just to forgive us our sins and to cleanse us from all unrighteousness. 1 John 1:9."

"I'm too thick," Baker protested, bowing his head. "What does it mean?"

She chose her words carefully, knowing that perhaps Tom Baker was indeed a doomed man. "Tell the Lord your sins."

"I got so many."

"Do you know what *faithful* means?"

"Reckon it's someone true to his word."

"Jesus is faithful. True unto death. What He promises, He will do. And here is His promise to you, Tom Baker. Confess your sins and He is true to His Word and will forgive you. Not only forgive you, but make you totally clean inside. Just as if you never sinned at all."

With these words, Baker bowed his head and began to weep again. "Oh thank you, ma'am! I been a'beggin' somebody to tell me what to do! I been askin' ever day and night! Oh Lord, Lord! What if I cain't recollect everything I done?"

She read the verse more slowly. "He is faithful and just to cleanse us from *all* unrighteousness."

"All," Baker repeated in wonder.

"Begin where you can. And ask God to take even the things you cannot recall. He is faithful."

With Eliza sitting at the top of the ladder, Tom Baker prayed and wept far into the night. There were petty crimes, lies, anger, blasphemy, and rebellion against his parents and God among his list of transgressions, but never did the murder of Nick Bledsoe come before the throne of the Almighty Faithful One.

When, at last, Tom Baker slumped to the floor in exhaustion and peace, Eliza was convinced that he was no murderer, nor was he a thief.

"Will you eat something now?" she queried.

"Yes'm," he croaked. "A glass of milk would be fine if it would not trouble you too much."

"I have cold fried chicken at the house."

"That would be real welcome, Mizz Richardson."

She hesitated only a moment before descending. "I'll be right back." She had no doubt that he would still be there when she returned with his supper.

I was dreaming of Eliza Richardson when the sound of her voice pulled me toward consciousness. As I struggled to sit up, a passage from *Paradise* Lost came to my mind. Adam dreamed that Eve had been created and when he awoke, he found her real.

Eliza Richardson was not Eve and Coloma was not Paradise. Yet, I fancied that she had miraculously gained a tender heart about me.

She called to me in a hoarse whisper, "Mister Ryland, I must have a word with you. I have information about the robbers."

I was instantly disappointed. Her call had nothing to do with a personal interest in me.

"What time is it?" I asked dully.

"Half past one, I think. It is urgent that we speak."

I groped to find my trousers and my boots in the dark. It came to me after a moment that I was still fully dressed and caked with sweat and dust from my exploits.

Stumbling to the door, I threw it open and invited her into my quarters. "You'll have to excuse . . ."

"That would not do at all, Mister Ryland. Not at this hour." Her response was indignant, as if it was I who had come calling on her uninvited instead of the other way around.

Stepping out into the chill of the autumn night brought me fully to my senses. "News about the robbers you say?" I could not make out her features in the starlight, but I smelled the sweet scent of lilac water on her skin.

"It's about Tom Baker." She said the name of the outlaw in an almost inaudible voice and then she glanced furtively over her shoulder as though she feared being overheard. "He could not have robbed the Georgetown stage."

I imagined that someone had discovered his body, cut it down from a tree, and brought it to the house of Doc Richardson. "He's at the end of a rope, no doubt," I said flatly.

She was silent a moment then said, "A bell rope to be precise."

"Poor devil." I leaned against the hitching rail and shook my head. "I suspected the jailbreak was staged for ill purposes."

"You are right on that count."

"Hung from the bell rope?"

"Found above the bell tower."

"In the church? Despicable. Entirely. I've been out beating the brush. It came to me that he would have barely had time enough to ride all the way to Georgetown to rob the stage. A lynch party had to be the only logical end for him."

"Go on." She encouraged me to continue with my conclusions.

I rubbed my aching forehead. "What I cannot understand is why one of the Georgetown outlaws referred to the band as the Tom Baker Gang. Or called himself by that name."

"Did he?" She was surprised by this scrap of information.

The explanation came to me in a flash. "Of course, one could have used Baker's name to mislead us. It makes sense, doesn't it? There is Tom Baker locked away in a cell, accused of being the leader of a band of cutthroats. If we all believe Baker is the mastermind behind the robbery and the one who killed Nick Bledsoe, then why should we look for the real villains?"

She snapped her fingers and gasped in comprehension. "You've hit it, Mister Ryland! Of course that's the explanation. Someone . . . right here in Coloma . . . knew that the Georgetown stage was about to be robbed. Tom Baker was set loose to mislead the law . . . and the rest of us, too. But Baker did not have the time or the means to get to Georgetown."

"Being dead, he could not have been there."

"What if he was alive?"

"Nearly impossible. A moot point at any rate, him being deceased."

"Is it moot?" She stepped closer. I could almost see her smile. There was amusement in her words.

"You said he was hanged."

"Suppose Tom Baker fled from the jail. Stumbled out into the darkness, ran into a clothesline . . ."

"Mister Marshall lost a blanket that night." It was plain she had somehow pieced together some of the details of the escape.

"Yes. I have seen Marshall's blanket."

I pictured the dead body of Baker wrapped in the blanket. "A pitiful sight."

"Indeed. Not much to keep a man warm."

"Not enough to warm a dead man." I can be remarkably thick at times.

She grasped my arm. "Mister Ryland, I have come for your help."

"Anything," I blurted.

"You must promise me . . ."

"Of course, Miss Richardson."

She stepped back from me and withdrew her hand. Her tone turned cold. "I have seen how much your promises are worth. Consider the case of the Bledsoe family."

The subject took such an abrupt turn that I was caught off guard. "Miss Richardson, I assure you I have not ceased to consider how I might fulfill my promise to come to the aid of the widow and orphans."

"I will hold you to that."

"My solemn oath."

"Good." The smile in her voice returned. "Then I ask you for your help in another matter. A matter of life and death."

"I am your servant." I bowed slightly and struck my hand against my breast.

"If I share a confidence with you, will you promise to tell no one?"

"As you wish."

Another pat on the arm. "Well, then. I believe everything you have said about Tom Baker. He is nothing but a pawn; a dupe in some larger game."

So we were back to Baker. "Thank you for your confidence." I did not know yet what she was getting at.

"Tom Baker had a mother and father in Georgia. He left them as a prodigal some three years ago. You must write them and tell them their son is innocent of the Wells, Fargo crimes, no matter what they may hear."

I assumed she had found some scrap of correspondence on the body. "Georgia is a long way off. I doubt they will hear anything about him one way or the other."

"Are you going back on your word?"

"No, ma'am!" I cried. "I'll do as you ask. And what shall I say about the death of their boy?"

"It's best to leave that for later."

"They've a right to know."

She turned and looked toward the sky in a long, thoughtful pause. "You must promise me that you will help me find out who is hiding behind Tom Baker's name . . . for he is the one who killed Nick Bledsoe and then devised a way for an innocent man to take the blame."

"I've made it my goal."

"Someone here in Coloma has betrayed us all in what he has done. We have to root him . . . or them . . . out. The way I see it, Mister Ryland, it will take brains and steady nerve to do it."

I sighed. She had inspired me to action against the villains who had framed Tom Baker and killed Nick Bledsoe and stolen my watch. "We will do it. Together, Miss Eliza." I did not know how we would do it and I was making promises by the dozen.

"Good." She seemed relieved at my earnestness. "Now that I have your word I will let you in on the secret that you must not share with another living soul." She slid her slender fingers down my arm and took my hand. "I dare not trust any other man with my news. Jim Hume would roar like the old Russian cannon beside the flagpole if he knew."

"I can keep my mouth shut."

"Well, then . . . I have seen Tom Baker."

"So you said. Poor fellow."

"He is alive, Mister Ryland."

I stammered, "But . . . but . . . you said . . ."

"He is innocent," she remarked more firmly. "You know it as surely as I do. He is innocent and he is wronged and he is alive!"

There was no question that Tom Baker would have to leave his hiding place at Emmanuel Church. The Methodist circuit rider was due to arrive in Coloma within a day. A dozen places of refuge were considered and each discarded in turn.

The calf pen in back of the Richardson house was out of the question. The milk cow would set up a fuss and Chin Lee would discover the fugitive within an hour. Eliza discussed the possibility of moving Baker to the attic of the school. It was decided that one misstep on a groaning rafter would arouse the curiosity of the students and the game would be up.

It was Eliza who came up with the one logical place in all of Coloma where no one would think to look for an escaped stage robber. That location was the small storage loft above my sleeping quarters in the Wells, Fargo office.

I objected, of course; expressing that this was something like hiding the fox in the chicken coop.

Eliza drew herself up in indignation at my remark. "He is no fox. He is an innocent man wrongly accused and in peril of his very life."

I had to agree that this was probably true. "But what if we are wrong about him? What if he is not an honest man? My responsibility is to . . ."

She cut me short. "I will stake my own life on the fact that he will not disappoint our expectations."

"And if he broke our confidence and robbed and plundered while I slept, how could you make good on such a wager?"

Her eyes narrowed. "Then ask me for whatever collateral I may offer as a personal pledge for his good behavior and complete trustworthiness."

The next words sprang from my mouth like the lines of a villain in a melodrama. "If he is not trustworthy . . . then you will marry me."

The stunned expression on her face betrayed first outrage and then dissolved into complete amusement. She fought back a smile; it broke through. She covered her mouth in an attempt to hold back her laughter. A small chuckle trickled out like water from a collapsing dam. A moment later the full roar of her laughter spilled out and engulfed me in embarrassment.

I blushed a deep crimson and remarked that I was only joking. Her laughter increased in volume.

"Marry you?" She coughed and wiped the tears of amusement from her eyes. "Something like winning a wife in a poker game, isn't it? Oh, Lord, Mister Ryland! You have cheered me up more than I can say!"

She must have seen my wounded expression. It is not every day, after all, that a man proposes matrimony even in the form of a wager. Patting me on the arm in a sisterly fashion, she shook her head, grinned broadly, and then extended her hand.

"If Tom Baker kills you in your sleep . . ." She paused. "That won't work, will it? I can't marry a dead man. All right then, if he coldcocks you and robs the Wells, Fargo office, I promise to marry you at the time and location of your choosing. In fact, I so trust him that I pledge that he will not steal at all."

I shook her outstretched hand and managed a half-hearted laugh. "You must be fully confident."

"I am," she said, and I knew she was.

This did not cheer me up. If Tom Baker proved to be a miscreant and stripped the office bare, I would lose my job and thus have no way to support my newly won bride. If he was completely pure as the driven snow, I would lose my bet and lose Eliza. Then it occurred to me that since Eliza was not mine, I could not really lose her.

I said, "Shall we draw up a contract?"

"I am good for my word." A wink. "As I am certain you are." Raising a finger into the air she changed the subject. "Speaking of which . . . Mister Ryland . . . you must bend your brains around the problem of raising support for the Bledsoe family."

"I was accomplished at college fund-raisers." I was grateful for the sudden leap from the subject of forced matrimony to the care of widows and orphans.

Her interest was sparked. "I suspected as much. You have the look of a fellow who would know his way around a box sociable."

Suspecting that this was an insult I defended myself. "Theater, Miss Richardson. I performed in several productions in my university days."

She sat back and gave the look of one impressed. "Theater! You are an actor, then?"

"Well, I . . ." Dare I admit my role as Ichabod Crane in the Princeton theater production of *The Legend of Sleepy Hollow*? "I have performed in an adaptation of Washington Irving's . . ."

"Washington Irving!" she gasped, truly impressed. "One of the greats! An adaptation, you say? Of what?"

I spoke the name of the work, even though we were getting dangerously near to one of my most embarrassing accomplishments.

She queried with some respect, "And did you write the play yourself?"

"I and a fraternity brother."

"And what part did you take?"

I swallowed hard. I tried to utter the name of the lanky and disgusting schoolmaster who courted the fairest female. "Crane," I admitted with less enthusiasm.

"Ah. Yes." She had the good grace not to scan my lanky form or remark on the fitness of the casting. Instead she said, "You are a sight more handsome than I imagined Ichabod Crane to be. I suppose with enough greasepaint . . ." She squeezed my hand and I felt better somehow. So she thought me a sight better looking than the beanpole of a schoolmaster. "Oh, Mister Ryland! The very idea sets me all alight! Do you suppose this is something you might re-create?"

"I can't say I want to re-create it." I resisted the horrific notion that I could get on stage and parade around in knickers and a pigtail and a tricornered hat. Every criminal in California would take me for a target if I did so! Wells, Fargo would average a robbery every day if the Coloma agent was to play such a part!

Eliza dismissed my fears. "But this is purest inspiration! The harvest festival is coming. A theatrical is the very thing! Then donate the proceeds to the Bledsoe family. You shall pen the script and I shall direct it. Together we must re-create your Princeton triumph!"

By the time Eliza Richardson left the office, I felt purely done in. She promised to return the next evening with Tom Baker in disguise and her copy of Washington Irving in hand.

I agreed to everything. I was her lackey in every way. After that encounter I believed myself to be a total idiot. My lunacy was the only truth I could be sure of.

I sat in my dark office and waited for Eliza to bring Tom Baker. The lamps of the Metropolitan Saloon winked out as the last drunk staggered through the swinging doors and onto the boardwalk. I was saddened but not surprised that this pathetic creature was none other than the famous Mr. Marshall, who had spent yet another evening in the tavern embellishing his account of how he had first discovered gold. Marshall's shy reticence when sober was in stark contrast to his effusive storytelling when in his cups.

The glow from the window of Magee's upstairs office pulled my gaze and intensified my unreasoning dislike of him. He was wide awake and counting his money, no doubt.

I glanced at the clock above the old desk. It was half past two in the morning. I turned the wick of my lamp lower, knowing that Eliza would wait until she was certain the town was asleep before she brought Tom Baker to me.

I was bone weary, but a sense of melancholy kept me from dozing off. I considered Marshall, staggering home toward his little shack from Magee's saloon each night. I thought of the pathetic wreck tending his pumpkin patch by day. Marshall had launched the great Gold Rush of '49 and yet now he lived in near poverty while others, like Magee, grew rich off his discovery.

How had Marshall sunk to such a condition in only a few short years? He earned his ration of whiskey at the Metropolitan by telling his tale of gold nuggets sparkling in the water of Sutter's Mill tailrace. Again and again Marshall recited the events while he stood at the bar of Magee's saloon. He attracted the greenhorns who came west to the goldfields looking for instant wealth. Unbeknownst to his most steady customer, Magee spread the rumor that Marshall had some divine gift for finding gold.

"And he's got a big cache buried somewhere in that pumpkin patch, I'll wager," Magee said often.

One look at Marshall's nightly condition should have struck down the fable, but still the travellers came to the Metropolitan to drink with the man who started the rush.

At the age of thirty-seven, Marshall's life was lived like that of a ghost. The glint of a gold nugget had lifted him from obscurity. Yet it had not freed him from failure and mediocrity. Marshall had only that one moment at Sutter's Mill to give meaning to his life. It was a flash of glory that he could not get beyond. Magee, who plied him with whiskey and kept him hanging around the saloon, made certain that Marshall would never be more than the last drunk out the door.

From my musings it came to me that there was something deeply disturbing about a man like Magee. He built his wealth upon the rubble of other men's lives. If he could do this, he was capable of abusing his authority in other ways. I was certain of it. I was again glaring hard at Magee's window when the soft tapping of Eliza's fist pulled me back to reality.

I called, "Who's there?"

Her voice was barely a whisper. "Open the door."

Dousing the light completely, I unlatched the door and opened it. The scent of lilac water preceded Eliza.

Tom Baker followed. He was clothed as a woman. His face was hidden by the brim of a large bonnet.

There was a moment of mute confusion as I gaped at this second female.

Eliza laughed at me and said, "If anyone happens to be snooping about at such an hour as this, word will be out tomorrow that you're a hypocritical scoundrel who likes his women large."

Baker cleared his throat nervously. A decidedly male cough. "Bless you, Mister Ryland. I hate to ruin the reputation of a fella who has done me such a good turn," he remarked in a deep bass as he removed the headgear.

I said, "My reputation will be a sight more ruined if anyone suspects that my visitor is not a lady of the night, but an accused night rider and publicly acclaimed murderer. There's a bedroll up in the attic. There's a chamber pot for you and water for drinking and water for washing and a tin of soda crackers if you fancy something to eat. But eat quietly and leave the dress on, Mister Baker, if you please. It will confuse all to thunder anyone who might come in here looking for trouble."

"I'm mighty thankful," Baker said, grasping my hand and pumping it as if he were hoping to draw water.

"Thank me best by not belching when someone comes through my door, nor blowing your nose. Not one peep or sigh if you please, Mister Baker, lest Miss Richardson and myself be hung with you."

Eliza promised to return with breakfast for two come morning. I remarked that morning was not so very far off and that she should be gone before Jim Hume spotted her, assumed I had soiled her good name, and killed me in retribution.

She grasped my arm, "Jim Hume may well have legitimate reason to wish you dead before we are finished. But I shall stand in the gap on your behalf, Mister Ryland. Never fear."

Leaving me with that cold comfort, she departed.

Everything in place, I lay down to sleep. Above my head the planks began to rattle. Tom Baker snored like a prize hog in the sun.

I must admit, I spent a very uneasy night.

CHAPTER 9

I caught up with Judge Magee the following morning. He was coming out of the side door of the Metropolitan and was evidently in some kind of hurry. He did not seem pleased to see me. "Ryland," he said curtly. "Lose any more prisoners lately?"

"No, sir, Your Honor," I replied gamely. "I've been trying to recover the one I lost." I told him briefly about my theory that Baker might have been lynched after all. "You must have suspected that, too, seeing as how you warned Ollie to be on his guard and sent him coffee and all."

"Yes, but thanks to your incompetence and that of that lamebrain . . . who should have been named Turniphead instead of Turnipseed . . . Baker escaped hanging altogether. You've been wasting time."

"Mighty certain of that, are you? You know, Your Honor," I continued. "Here's something I've been wondering about: there have been no reports of stolen horses. Not from Creedmore, not from anybody in town, unless they just don't feel like mentioning it. How do you figure Baker got clean away so fast?"

"Isn't it obvious?" Magee said scornfully. "His gang brought an extra mount with them when they busted him out. You just don't want to admit that he was as guilty as sin and you are responsible for his successful flight."

I nodded slowly and Magee took this as a sign of contrite submission. He had one foot up in the stirrup of his tall, high-strung yellow gelding when I stopped him with another observation. "Those horses must have all had wings, then."

It is awkward to be caught half on and half off a horse. There should be a smooth motion to swinging a leg over a saddle once it gets started. The combination of a moment's hesitation and a fractious horse and any pretense to grace is lost.

"What do you mean?" Magee demanded. His voice burbled a little with the jostling of his mount.

I waited till the palomino had stopped dancing and Magee had more or less centered his potbelly over the horn. "Ollie said he got his coffee from Pedro around midnight. That means the break was some later than that. Now the Georgetown stage was robbed just after two in the morning. Two hours will take a man from here to Georgetown on a good horse . . . but only just barely . . . and the robbery was up the road a good distance farther than that."

"See here, Ryland," Magee scolded. "What are you suggesting?"

"I'm suggesting that even if Tom Baker escaped from the cell and was not lynched, he still could not have been the same man as held up the Georgetown stage."

"The explanation is still simple." Magee sounded exasperated, as if he were lecturing a particularly backward child on some elementary lesson. "Part of the gang released Baker, while the rest robbed the stage. Then they met up later."

Shaking my head provoked Magee even more. "Only it didn't happen that way. I found where all seven gang members waited for the coach and I followed the man who held up Macreedy from that very spot."

"What would be the purpose of using Baker's name then? You yourself reported that Macreedy was robbed by a man calling himself Tom Baker. What would be the sense of that?"

"That's just what I've been wondering, Judge," I said. "Good day to you." I slapped the gelding on the rump and Magee cantered down Main Street and out of town.

The meadow beside the American River was quiet and carpeted with lush green grass. The warmth of the day was enough to drive the mosquitoes into the shade under the willows, but not so great as to make the swale unpleasant.

All in all, it was a perfect setting. It was an ideal place and time to forget the fact that I had a wanted murderer hiding in my office, and to forget the two stage robberies for which Wells, Fargo was demanding solutions. I could even temporarily put out of my mind my folly in agreeing to re-create my most hated experience: Ichabod Crane!

That commitment I could not ignore very much, however. The other party to the contract was very near indeed. Every time Eliza leaned toward me, the scent of lilacs wafted into my senses like the wisps of cottonwood fiber drifting on the breeze.

"Pay attention, Mister Ryland," Eliza snapped. "How do you expect to become any kind of marksman without concentrating?"

Her perfume may have savored of dreams, but her tone was reminiscent of the classroom. And I was the errant pupil!

"This is a breech-loading Lovell shotgun, the same as carried by Wells, Fargo guards," she instructed. "The lever on the stock opens the breech." She suited her action to the words. "You load a cloth pouch of shot in each chamber and follow with one paper pouch of powder. Tear a small hole in the paper as you load it." She snapped the breech closed. "Pull the hammers back to the half-cock safety position and apply the percussion caps."

Her ears were like perfectly formed seashells.

"Mister Ryland! Are you listening?"

"What? Oh, yes, Miss Richardson. Percussion caps . . . safety."

Even though coming unconsciously to my lips, the correct phrases mollified her some. "Just so," she said. "Now, over on those rocks I have placed a row of pinecones. I want you to shoot them off."

"Now?"

"Yes, Mister Ryland," Eliza replied with a touch of asperity. "Before they drop their seeds and the trees that result are too thick to shoot through."

She stepped back behind me and covered her ears with her hands.

The weapon I held was truncated in both barrel and stock. This was done on purpose to make it quicker in use, but prevented me from raising it to my shoulder. "Hold the weapon so that it shoots where you are looking," she shouted. "Hang on tight and squeeze the trigger."

The shotgun leaped in my hands, my head rang with the report and . . . to my gratification, the cone disintegrated! Without waiting for instruction, I rotated my hips, swung the scattergun around, and blasted away again. This time the cone jumped high up in the air and swirled off into the river.

"Bravo, Mister Ryland," Eliza applauded. "You and a shotgun seem to be made for each other."

"Tennis," I commented.

"Tennis?" she repeated.

"Yes. My college experience included lawn tennis. Very good for hand and eye coordination."

I spent the rest of the afternoon practicing loading and firing until I could reload both barrels in under a minute. Then we went on to moving targets, with Eliza skimming pie tins into the air. I got so I could hit four out of five, regardless of where they were thrown or where I was looking when she launched them.

I should point out that we did not target practice all afternoon. At one point we had a picnic lunch of cold fried chicken.

The morning air had the tang of frost in it. I was curled up in my blankets, endeavoring to keep all my length under the covers. If I stretched out, my feet and half my shins hung over the edge of the cot.

I was making a good job of it though, and dreaming of Eliza when the door of the Wells, Fargo office rattled under an insistent fist. "Ryland!" Jim Hume's voice bellowed. "Get up!"

A quick glance at the wall clock told me that it lacked ten minutes of being five o'clock. Probably not a social call, then. I doubted if even as blunt a man as Jim Hume would choose the hour before dawn to discuss his prior claim to Miss Richardson. Official business, then.

"Hold on," I yelled back. "I'm coming!" In a hoarse whisper I hissed to Baker, "Keep still! As you value your neck, keep still!" I could only hope that the boisterous knocking had awakened my upstairs guest. What if he was still asleep and snored right over the head of Deputy Hume?

When I unlatched the door Hume burst in. Behind him was Tim Flynn and behind Flynn were a half dozen others. "We've got a lead at last," Hume said without preamble. "At least part of the gang is denned up right where we figured, on the north side of the river, over around Michigan Bluff." As I dressed, Hume filled me in on the details. "I've got an informant over there, who says a deserted cabin suddenly has occupants."

"Is that it?" I asked, hunting for a missing sock and finding it under the safe. Apprehensive that Baker would somehow give himself away, I started hopping toward the door with my boots in my hand. "Why is that SO STARTLING?" I said in an overloud tone.

"By itself, it isn't," Hume admitted, looking at me strangely since I was almost shouting. "But there's more. A man showed up in town to buy supplies, for him and a partner, he said. Paid in gold coin, and bought enough beef and beans for half a dozen men. Expensive things, too; tinned oysters, fresh eggs."

I managed to propel the early morning callers out onto the boardwalk. "Imagine that," I commented. It was difficult to divide my attention between covering for Baker and actually listening to Hume's words.

Perhaps it is in my nature to be argumentative, but I still was unconvinced that this was not some wild-goose chase. "Could be some greenhorn with cash to spread around."

Hume shook his head. "Man who bought the goods said he would pick them up next day. Well, the storekeeper was headed down toward the old cabin anyway and took the order along. When he got in sight of the place he saw enough clothes drying for six or seven men and that many horses in the corral."

In the middle of this explanation, Tim Flynn disappeared. Maybe he had heard it all before, but his absence was no hair off my hide.

Yanking up my tall boot by the mule ears I stomped it into place. "Worth looking into," I said at last.

"One more thing," Hume added. "Before the storekeeper got within fifty yards of the place, the buyer rushed out and stopped him . . . made him unload the supplies in the barn and watched till the clerk drove out of sight."

"Bingo!" I said. "Something going on there they don't want anybody to know about. This rich purchaser didn't have a raspy voice by any chance?"

"No," Hume replied. "I asked that, too. He was a young man, fair-haired, clean-shaven, and nothing remarkable about his speech."

"Do you have the list of what was bought?" I asked on a sudden impulse.

"Right here," Hume said, passing over a page torn from a receipt book.

I scanned it quickly, noting that whoever these men were, they ate a sight better than I. Then, near the bottom in a cramped pencil scrawl was the entry I had been seeking. Holding it pinched between finger and thumb, I turned the paper so Hume could read the words "1 dz Raleigh Five Star."

"Mean something?" Hume asked.

"Maybe," I started to explain. "Twice before . . ."

At that moment Tim Flynn returned and with him was Judge Magee. I clammed up and, to my relief, Hume did not ask me to continue. Instead he addressed the judge. "Well, Your Honor," he said. "What brings you out so early?"

"Is it true that you're on to the gang?"

Hume shrugged, a gesture that lacked the enthusiasm with which he had pounded on my door. "Could be," he said guardedly. "A lead to follow up."

"I'm riding along," Magee stated flatly.

"That is hardly necessary," Hume argued. The lawman was polite but that was all. "We already have the warrants and . . ."

"There are two ways justice can miscarry," Magee said. I watched Hume's spine stiffen at the lecturing tone of the judge's voice. "One is for an innocent man to be punished and the other is for the guilty to go free. I will not allow the good name of El Dorado County to be sullied by newspapers attacking the competence of our legal process. And I am coming along."

Jim Hume's jaw clenched and I thought he was going to argue, but all he said was, "Mount up then."

Using the excuse that I needed to collect my shotgun, I returned to the empty back room. With an eye on the group of men outside the front window I hissed, "Don't move more'n you have to. I'll be back quick as I can. Maybe this will clear you. Do you hear me?"

A muffled grunt of assent told me Baker had heard.

When the posse was all gathered on horseback at the north end of town, Hume added one further word. "If these men are the ones we seek, then they are armed and will not be taken easily. Are all of you prepared for whatever comes?"

It was easier to nod than to speak, and I patted the shotgun in the scabbard by my right hand. Flynn and the others checked their weapons and off we went.

━━━◆━━━

It was a whale of a ride. Even Ophelia caught the excitement of the chase and increased her pace to match the younger, spryer mounts of the others. We descended into the gorge of the middle fork, through oaks to scrub brush and buckthorns, across a rocky ford and up the other side. Once on the northern bank we ascended even farther than we had dropped, climbing past the oaks again to the black locusts and digger pines.

It was late afternoon before we wound our way up a tableland and onto Michigan Bluff. In a dusty clearing no more remarkable than a hundred others, Hume stopped the posse and had us gather around. "We're close," he said. "No more than a mile up this canyon. We're splitting into two groups here. Magee, Ryland, and Flynn with me. Ollie, you and the others circle around and close the back door while we knock on the front."

"Why let that old geezer lead? Why don't I take the second group?" Flynn protested. "As it is I'll wind up nursemaid to the crybaby here." He was referring to me, of course, but Hume did not buy it.

"Flynn, you've crossed me once too often and I want you where I can keep an eye on you. Any back talk and you can cut out for home right now, savvy?" I wondered if the idea of keeping an eye on folks applied to Judge Magee as well, but it did not seem polite to ask. "Now you men," Hume addressed Ollie's group, "get going. Spread 'em around both slopes, Ollie, and give me a whistle when you're in place."

No matter my differences with Jim Hume, I admired what he was doing for Ollie Turnipseed. The guard, who still felt the weight of letting Tom Baker escape, straightened up and squared his shoulders. "You can count on me, Jim," Ollie said. "Let's go."

"Now," Hume addressed us when Ollie's group had departed, "here's the plan. We ride easy up to the edge of the clearing. I'm going to try to talk them out. Is that clear?" His words applied to us all, but he was staring at Flynn when he spoke. Flynn gave a curt nod. "All right, then," Hume concluded. "Check your pieces. Spread out in a line behind me and keep back. Stop when I tell you."

There was a screen of mullein stems just beyond where the trees stopped. The seven-foot-tall spikes had dropped their yellow blossoms, but the javelinlike stalks were covered in reddish purple hairs. From some part of my college years I dredged up the memory that these plants were called "hag tapers," since witches were supposed to use them as torches for their midnight rites. It was not the best association to recollect right before confronting a gang of outlaws.

Anyway, the mullein spikes made a fence of sorts that shielded the cabin from view but also hid us from sight. Hume stopped us there and had us dismount and wait.

Through small gaps in the growth I saw a tumble-down barn and a corral with three horses in it. Beyond that was a one-story log cabin. A thin curl of smoke drifted lazily up into the sky.

The wait was not long. A particularly loud-voiced quail whistled "Chi-ca-go, Chi-ca-go," and was answered by Hume. "Keep back," he said to us again, while he parted the screen of plants and stepped out. "Holloa the cabin," he called out. "This is Deputy Jim Hume. I want you to all come out so I can ask you some questions. Make it quick!"

There was no response at first, then the front door opened about an inch. "What d'ya want?"

"Come out with your hands up!" Hume ordered.

"Go away!" the man shouted back. "We got the cholera here. Keep back!"

"Is that so?" Hume retorted. "I believe I'll take my chances. Now, just so we're clear on how things stand, this cabin is surrounded by my men. There is no chance of escape. Come out peaceably and you'll live. I can't vouch for anything else!"

That challenge was the signal to open the ball, as the westerners said. A rifleshot from the hayloft of the barn kicked up dirt between Jim Hume's boots. They had a sentry posted! Hume dived for cover. I saw the lookout's rifle barrel swing after him for another try.

Rising from behind the hag tapers, I pivoted the shotgun and fired it from the hip. The first blast tore a chunk out of the wall of the barn about the size of a pinecone. When I caught the glint of light on the rifle barrel again, I let fly with the second load of buckshot and the marksman jumped back.

We were drawing fire from the house now, pistol bullets whining past my ears. One of the outlaws shot from the front door and the other blasted away from a hole in a shuttered window. I followed Hume's example and jumped behind a mound of earth that suddenly seemed none too high and none too thick.

"Thanks," Hume breathed. "You gave me a chance to get down. I did not expect them to be on the shoot so quick."

"Where's Flynn?" I asked, looking around. "And Magee?"

Both of our partners had disappeared with the first fusillade. Whether they were behind a substantial tree or angling for a better place to return the fire, I could not say.

A steady hail of bullets came into the back of the cabin from Ollie's men at the rear. It had only been a minute since the first shot was fired and already the air hung thick with the stink of gunsmoke. "Hold your fire!" Hume yelled into the first momentary lull. "Will you surrender now?"

For answer his words drew the renewed attention of all three guns. Stalks of mullein were splintering and flying around us as if a giant scythe were going through a cornfield.

I had reloaded the shotgun and rose to one knee to fire again when a slug pinged off the stock just behind my left hand. The impact knocked the gun from my hands. "Keep down and scoot back," Hume said, indicating that we should withdraw a ways to deeper cover.

There was a tree stump nearby and a boulder rolled against it. The two formed a notch lined up with the front door of the shanty. Through this crevice I poked the shotgun, but the angle was too low. I would still have to expose myself to get off a useful shot.

Watching from behind my makeshift fort, I noticed that the bandit who fired from the doorway closed the panel when he withdrew to reload. To Hume I said, "Keep the one in the barn off me." I counted six shots, then six more from another pistol, then the front door swung shut.

The seconds went by slowly while the reloading was going on. So much time passed, in fact, that I thought my plan was a bust and the sniper moved to another position.

The instant the door panel quivered I jumped up and shouted to Hume, "Now!" From his rifle a steady stream of bullets pounded the upper floor of the barn, driving the lookout back. At the same moment I loosed both barrels into the front door of the cabin. Splinters from the frame flew in all directions and the door flung open.

In the exchange of fire, Jim Hume caught a bullet in the shoulder. Whether it came from the second man in the cabin or the one in the barn, I could not say. It spun him around and worse yet, dropped him out in the open; an easy mark.

That is when I saw Ollie Turnipseed run full tilt around the corner of the cabin. He was on a line with the gates of the barn. He discharged one barrel of his shotgun into the shutters of the cabin, then the other load up toward the loft. "No, Ollie!" I yelled. "Stay back!"

"Get Jim!" was his shout of reply. Throwing away the scattergun, Ollie drew a revolver from his belt and continued shooting. He was drawing the fire from us and giving me a chance to rescue the deputy.

It worked. I gathered Hume to me in a swoop and the two of us rolled and tumbled back behind the boulder, just as another bullet shattered on the rock no more than a foot above my head.

When I peered out of the crevice again, Ollie was trapped in the yard with no cover. The gates of the barn were bolted and as he turned to run, his knees buckled and he sagged to the dirt.

Hume's wound was not serious. The slug had creased the top of his shoulder and plowed a bloody furrow. He gritted his teeth as I shoved a bandana under his collar and pressed his right hand down on top of the wound. "Hold that," I ordered. Then I returned to the battle.

The outlaw in the barn already had his fill. No more shots came from the loft. A small movement caught my eye and a board moved just above the ground. Then a man-shape, blonde-haired, hunched over, and crawling, ducked behind a corral post. "Flynn, Magee," I yelled, not even knowing if they were anywhere around to respond. "Behind the barn! He's making a break!"

As if my words were the starter's gun of a race, the outlaw vaulted the four-rail corral fence, scattered the horses, and made for the far side. I loosed two shots in his direction, knocking the tops off fence posts like blowing out birthday candles, but failing to stop him. If anything, the near misses spurred the fugitive on to greater speed. He cleared the last fence of the corral without even touching the rail. Only a dozen yards of open ground separated him from thick chaparral and escape.

Another bullet fired by the remaining outlaw in the cabin filed a groove in the stump directly in line with my head. If it had not turned aside on a knot, I would not have been around to witness the rest of the conflict. As it was, I could not stay under cover and reload quickly enough to make any difference. It seemed that the fleeing bandit was going to get away.

Out of the brush to my left popped Tim Flynn. Charging toward the outlaw from the side, he was firing his Colt as he went.

Attacked from this unexpected quarter, the blonde-haired man shoved a revolver under his left arm and shot at Flynn as he ran. Flynn jogged aside and returned the fire.

I saw the blonde man stumble, then drop his gun. Flynn shot again and it looked as though an unseen hand lifted the fugitive by the back of his shirt and flipped him head over heels. He tumbled to a sprawling stop, his right arm draped over a clump of buckthorn as if claiming victory in his race.

There was an interval of silence then when all shooting stopped. I felt a tug on my sleeve from behind and almost knocked Jim Hume's head off with the double barrel as I spun around.

"Lemme up there," he said. His face was pale and his voice reedy, but he hauled himself determinedly over to the stump. Hume attempted to call out to the remaining outlaw, but his voice would not carry above a few feet. "You do it," he urged me. "Take charge. Get him to surrender."

I stuck his hat on top of a stick and thrust it into the air to attract the attention of the remaining gunman. "You in the cabin," I shouted. "You've lost this hand. Give up now and you won't get hurt."

"Not a chance," a voice from the shanty replied. "You ain't gonna stretch my neck. If you want me, come and get me!"

Hume nudged me and shook his head. He thought I was making a pretty feeble job of it. Getting the last bandit to see reason was not going to be as easy as I thought. I resorted to more persuasive words. "There's twenty of us out here with plenty of ammunition and a bucket of kerosene. Don't make me set fire to the place . . . 'cause if I do, we're shooting anybody who comes out alive. What'll it be?"

When I turned to look at Hume for approval he had a look of shock and surprise on his face. Then he nodded and smiled at me.

The door creaked open and an arm in a bloody shirt-sleeve appeared, waving a pair of long handles. "Don't shoot," a voice croaked. "You've killed Poole. And where's Gillespie?" The question referred to the lookout who had run from the barn.

"He made a break for it, but he's dead," I said. "Throw your weapon through the door and come out with your hands up."

You won't gun me down?"

"Listen!" I shouted to the posse. "This is Ryland. Everybody hold your fire! He's coming out and I don't want any shooting. Flynn, see to Ollie."

A rifle was tossed out of the barricaded shack. It pitchpoled on its muzzle, then flopped in the gravel.

I helped Hume to his feet. He leaned against the stump, swaying slightly. "Go get him," he said. "He's your prisoner . . . you did good."

The walk toward the cabin across the open dusty ground, with the dead body of Gillespie lying in the weeds and Flynn bending over the doubled-up form of Ollie by the barn, was the longest stroll I have ever taken. I kept the shotgun cradled in my arms and pointed toward the cabin door, but I was the one out in the open with nowhere to hide.

A bull-like, thick-necked man appeared in the entry. One of his arms dangled at his side and in the other he held the flag of surrender. "Don't shoot me," he said again. "I give up."

"Nobody's gonna shoot you," I reassured him. "Step out here where I can see you."

My captive advanced three steps past the shadow of the overhang and stood blinking in the sunlight. His face was streaked with blood and smoke.

A figure came out of the bushes to my right. At first I did not know which of the posse it was. There was a loud clicking noise as the newcomer cocked a pistol. In the tense stillness of the afternoon, the latching of the hammer was enough to attract the attention of the surrendering outlaw.

The last robber pivoted at the noise and his eyes widened. "Judge," he said. "You . . ."

There was a roar of gunfire and the pistol in Judge Magee's hand bucked upward. The bandit clutched his chest and dropped to both knees. "Hold your fire!" I screamed, running forward. "Hold your fire!"

Blood spreading across his shirt, the outlaw reached out his arm toward the judge, who thumbed back the hammer and fired again. The man fell forward onto his face and never moved again.

I was moving too fast to stop. I barrelled into Magee with my head and shoulders, sending his six-gun flying and knocking him over backward. I followed, grabbing him by the coat collar and jerking him upright. "I said don't shoot!" I screamed into his face.

"He was going for a gun," Magee protested. "Ask Flynn."

I turned to see Flynn bending over the body of the outlaw. "The judge is right," he said, holding up a small, two-barrelled pistol. "He was carrying a hideout gun. Prob'ly gonna make you a hostage when you got close enough. Judge Magee saved your life."

"And killed the last hope we had of getting a lead on the rest of the gang," Jim Hume said, joining the knot of men clustered around the dead man. "You know, Judge," Hume said with steely eyes. "I believe this fella recognized you."

"Of course he did," Magee blustered, retrieving his pistol. "And I recognize him, too. Name's Will something-or-other. Known as Downieville Will . . . a small-time cattle rustler. I've seen paper on him before."

So that was the battle of Michigan Bluff. Three outlaws dead. Inside the cabin we discovered gold bars and coins that proved beyond doubt that these had been part of the gang that robbed the stage. We were no closer to resolving the mystery of Tom Baker, capturing the remaining outlaws, or recovering the rest of the loot.

Ollie Turnipseed, bless his thick hide, lived. The slug he had taken lodged in the gristle of his back. It had glanced off his hipbone and turned aside into the muscle, without doing serious harm. The shock had blacked him out, but he was not in danger. We secured a wagon and took him back to Coloma and Doc Richardson. When Ollie protested against having to ride in the buckboard with three corpses, I quit worrying about him.

CHAPTER 10

A few days after the shootout at Michigan Bluff, Eliza delivered breakfast for me and Tom Baker just after sunup. She pledged to have some good news for me about some old friends of mine who were willing to help with the Bledsoe matter. She would not tell me which old friends or if they planned to help solve the murder or assist in some other way. When I pressed her for an explanation, she smiled coyly and left as quickly as she had come.

Biscuits, gravy, scrambled eggs, fried potatoes, and a thick slice of apple-cured ham steamed before me. I could hear the clank of Baker's fork against the tin plate.

"Hold it down, will you?" I snapped. The rattle quieted some and just in time, too.

A heavy fist pounded against the door of the front office. My mornings were always getting interrupted, it seemed. On reflection, so did my nights and my days.

Through a mouthful of ham I choked out a harsh whisper. "Somebody's here!"

Dead silence from the loft.

The pounding echoed in my swirling brain. How much longer was I going to be able to keep up the front that all was well when I had a wanted man in my attic?

I raised the shade on the window and felt the blood drain from my face. I boomed cheerfully in an attempt to give warning to Baker, "WELL, WELL, LOOK HERE! IT'S DEPUTY JIM HUME!"

Opening the door, I stepped aside and let Hume pass.

"Morning, Ryland," he said in a distracted tone. He raised his nose and sniffed the delicious aroma of Eliza's cooking.

"MORNING, HUME!" I patted him too vigorously on the back. "FINE MORNING!" He must have thought I was half deaf in the mornings and raised my voice to compensate.

Hume did not return my good cheer. He spotted the heaping platter of food. "I thought you were supposed to eat at the boardinghouse." He did not approve of me having my morning meal in the office, that was plain enough.

I gulped. Would Hume recognize that the eggs were cooked by his beloved? By the girl he fancied to be his? Would he spot those biscuits and run me through or run me out of town on a rail or perhaps just shoot me? Never mind that a fugitive was sweating in the loft. Breakfast served by Eliza Richardson was ten times more a crime in the eyes of the smitten deputy.

I decided I did not care. "I took a fancy to Miss Richardson's cooking in my short stay at their place. I asked for another breakfast and . . ."

"Eliza's cooking? Eliza can't cook a thing except maybe an apple pie once in a while. If Eliza cooked this you'd be chewing into the next century. You have been deceived." He picked up a biscuit and took an enormous bite. Closing his eyes in bliss he spoke around the mouthful. "Ling made that. I'd know the smell of Ling's biscuits if you blindfolded me and led me for a hundred miles and took me into her kitchen and asked me where I was. The best." He finished off the morsel. "Just saw Eliza. She tells me you're going to be an actor. Put on a theatrical. Sleepy Hollow, eh? You're just right for it, I told her. You're just the one for it."

"All right. All right." I was chagrined. "You're here early. Is this business or did you come to eat my breakfast and gloat?"

"Got a burr under your saddle, Ryland?" Hume dug into the pocket of his mackinaw and pulled out my father's watch. "Thought you might like to have this back. Found it on one of the dead men."

I took it and held it to the morning light. I was glad to have it.

"Which dead man?"

"The one Magee shot. The fellow you promised long life and prosperity to. Thought getting your watch back might cheer you up some, considering that Eliza intends to put you on public display with that acting troupe that just came into town . . ."

"Acting troupe?"

"Hampton Theatric something. A couple of floosies and their dandies. Old friends of yours, I hear? You bought your horse from them."

"Not them," I defended weakly. "It was the livery fellow who . . . well, the company seem decent enough people."

"I reckon. Considering they intend to hold you up to ridicule so as you won't be able to show your face in these parts again."

"You did come to gloat."

Hume's face hardened with his perceived victory. "You did me a good turn at the bluff and I won't forget it. But . . ." there was a long pause that said life and limb were one thing while romance was altogether different. "You might have some ideas about her, fancy man, but after this nonsense, you're finished here."

"I still have a job to do."

"Ichabod," he said smirking. "Bible name, ain't it? The glory is departed, I believe it means."

"She might not have cooked the eggs, but she brought them to me."

The expression of victory remained fixed. "She doesn't want her star player bolting before opening night, that's all." Hume clapped me on the back. "I admit you had me worried. But not now. I know my girl."

"Thanks for the watch. Now my ham is getting cold."

Hume winked and snatched a second biscuit. "Your ham all right."

Watching him cross the street and saunter toward the jail, I spotted the wagon of the Hampton Theatrical Company at the same instant Hume burst into laughter, which echoed among the listening hills.

A sense of humiliation washed over me. Was Eliza only trying to butter me up so I would not run out on her plans?

The ceiling groaned. I glanced up. "He's gone," I remarked to the rafters.

The meek voice of my unwanted guest replied, "Mizz Eliza thinks highly of you. Don't believe that feller."

"How would you know?" I snapped.

"She said there ain't nobody but you she'd trust in all this, Mister Ryland. That's a fact. She said you was the only one and never mind who baked them biscuits, neither."

I muttered, "Trust. Well, yes. She probably trusts her grandmother, too, but a lot of good trust will do me."

"Don't you worry none." The clank of spoon against plate resumed happily. "I'd bet my life on you." A small chuckle. "I guess I have done it, ain't I?"

It was actually Jim Hume's teasing that gave me the idea. Maybe I do my best thinking when I'm angry. In this instance, being mortified as I was over Hume's badgering made something click in my brain.

I could hardly wait to knock on Eliza's door. "Show me the garden," I said with a wink, wanting to get out of earshot of the house.

"All right," she agreed with a puzzled look. She emerged a moment later wearing a floppy-brimmed straw hat and toting a basket. Eliza escorted me through a review of the late harvest corn. "What is it?" she said at last. "You are practically wiggling like a puppy."

I thought I had been hiding my emotions rather well and said so.

"Please, Mister Ryland," Eliza laughed. Plucking an ear of corn, she added it to her basket. "It is not possible for someone as tall and striking as you to not be noticed when his face is shining like the beacon of a lighthouse."

From her this sounded good, and not at all like the heckling of Jim Hume.

"All right," I said. "Here goes. What two problems do we have?"

"Seeing that Tom Baker is acknowledged as innocent and set free is one."

"And the other?"

"Providing for the Bledsoes by way of the theatrical benefit performance."

"Exactly." I applauded. "Now, is there any reason that we could not accomplish both purposes in one night? What if we spread the word about how much money will be in Coloma on that one night . . . thousands of dollars, maybe."

"Why that would be asking to be robbed," she scolded and then stopped. Her hand shot up to her mouth.

"Precisely," I said. "Perhaps we can draw the so-called Baker Gang right into our grasp. Instead of waiting for them to strike elsewhere and running all over the countryside afterward, what say we make them come to us?"

Eliza was pleased at my thought, but cautious as well. "Let us see how much excitement the benefit performance generates for its original purpose before we give it another task as well," she warned. "How will you drum up enthusiasm for two-dollar tickets to a theatrical display?"

I could feel my grin widening, knew that she saw it, and I did not even mind. "Just leave that to me," I said. "Only, when I come to school next, don't argue if I ask to borrow your pupils."

It felt good to me that besides the five Bledsoe siblings, I was also being assisted by most of the other schoolchildren of Coloma. As I passed round handfuls of bright yellow posters and tacks, there was no teasing about who was a beggar. In fact, the only competition was who could distribute the papers the fastest and return for more.

GREAT HARVEST FESTIVAL THEATRICAL
PERFORMANCE

the handbill read.

WORLD-RENOWNED ACTING TROUPE BRINGS WORK
OF BEST-LOVED AMERICAN AUTHOR TO COLOMA
STAGE FOR ONE NIGHT ONLY!

The posters were topped with the looming figure of the Headless Horseman; a black-draped form that towered over a coal-black stallion. Jets of flame shot from the horse's eyes and mouth. Under the arm of the decapitated apparition was a grinning jack-o'-lantern. Beams of light also darted from the pumpkin's wicked eyes and leering mouth.

Eve Bledsoe was too little to carry posters, but her next older sister tugged my sleeve. "Pleath, Mithter Ryland, can I have thome more to put up?" she lisped.

"Certainly, Danette," I agreed. "But doesn't the picture of the horseman scare you?"

"Oh," she said. "I don't look. I carry them upthide down and clothe my eythes when I tack them."

She illustrated this method by adding a handbill to the front of the livery stable, despite the fact that it already possessed seventeen of them.

Within three hours of starting, all the walls, trees, hitching rails, water troughs, and outhouses of Coloma were festooned with flyers. *The Legend of Sleepy Hollow* was everywhere, as was the information that the proceeds would benefit the Bledsoe family.

What was more, Adam Bledsoe and the older boys decorated all the roadside trees between Placerville and Georgetown and clear up into the listening hills. With a week to go before the performance, there was no way one could be alive in El Dorado County and not know about the play.

There were two levels of planning that went on. The first involved the actors and the townspeople of Coloma, who saw only the preparations for the play and the Harvest Festival. What they also knew, because I talked about it everywhere, was how much money would be brought into Coloma for that one night.

Before long I was hearing exaggerated versions of my own expansive account. When I went to James Marshall's cabin to contract for a number of his largest pumpkins, he said, "I hear tell there'll be more gold in town come performance night than any time since the Rush. You figger on bringing in ten thousand dollars that one evening, is that so?"

I allowed that I had heard that amount mentioned.

"Dang," Marhsall said. "You be on your guard, then. Sums like that will pull desperate characters into town."

Such was exactly my hope.

The second level of planning took place with much greater secret deliberations and in a more select group. Only Eliza and Tom Baker were in my confidence. I did not even tell my fellow performers, for fear that one slip would give the game away.

"But you have to tell Jim Hume," Eliza urged. "He's got to know and be ready to help. We can't do this alone."

"I know," I admitted. "But convincing Jim to go along with this will be tough enough. Plus, I still can't let on about my upstairs roommate."

Eliza squeezed my arm. "You'll manage it," she said. "I believe in you."

I floated away toward my office in a cloud that was not entirely composed of yellow handbills.

———◇———

A pair of dark green oak leaves chased each other in the swirl of an autumn breeze. The spicy aroma of baking pumpkin pies drifted down the street from the Sierra Nevada Hotel. Despite the strong attraction of a warm slice of pie and a fragrant cup of coffee, Jim Hume and I were deep in conversation and walking along Main Street in the opposite direction.

"You still don't get it," I complained to Hume. "There is nothing that can possibly go wrong."

"Sure there is," he retorted. "Offhand, I can think of at least a dozen things. Besides, what makes you think that Baker's gang would ride into something that looks right on the face of it like a made-to-order ambush?"

I launched into the third time of trying to explain my scheme. "Think about them hitting another stage so soon after Nick Bledsoe's killing," I said. "Think about stopping during a getaway to rob poor old Macreedy." To myself I added the thought that Baker or one of his henchmen had been in Coloma and arranged to spring the Tom Baker I knew, just so as to make certain he was thought guilty. But of course I could not relay this notion to Hume without getting uncomfortably near the fact that Baker was still *in* Coloma. So what I concluded with was this: "The leader of the gang is convinced of his own invincibility. The fact that he escaped the shoot-out at Michigan Bluff reinforced that idea, but also gave him the added motive of revenge."

Hume pushed his hat up his high forehead and studied me with thoughtful eyes. "So give me the details again."

This was the first time he had not flatly refused to admit any merit to my scheme, so I swallowed my impatience and began anew. "We advertise all over the county that a special theater performance will be given as a benefit for Missus Bledsoe and the kids. That'll bring out everybody in the hills at two bits a head . . . maybe a thousand of them. We also let it be known around that Wells, Fargo has put up another thousand dollars for the capture of Baker and that the reward money is in town."

"Now hold it right there," Hume warned, holding up a cautionary finger. "That's reason enough for anybody who knows Baker to betray him. Won't that keep him away from town?"

"Not this man," I argued. "Besides, we already know he has an informant in Coloma. Someone who has an ear to the whereabouts of you and the posse."

"Flynn?" Hume guessed aloud. "Or Magee?"

It flattered me that the deputy had at last taken me into his confidence. It also pleased me that my thinking and his matched so completely. "Or they could be in cahoots."

Hume smiled as the westernism rolled off my Eastern tongue. "Then we keep them both in the dark."

"Yes," I agreed. "But not completely."

"What do you mean?"

I drew Jim Hume over to the lee of a water oak covered in posters and scanned the surroundings for listeners. Finding none, I continued. "If we tell them nothing at all, then that will make them suspicious and the word will surely reach Baker's gang. It would put the wind up them for certain. So instead of that, you take them into your confidence."

Hume fairly exploded. "I do what?"

"Take them aside privately. Tell them you've got word that Baker's gang has moved again and holed up . . . I dunno . . . way below the South Fork, say . . . and that you'll be on their trail. Tell them to be especially watchful of any strangers in town."

"And then I ride out with enough supplies to be gone a month," Hume said, warming to the idea. "And sneak back some night. I get in at midnight and hole up in your office."

"NO!" It was my turn to respond louder than necessary. Quickly I recovered and said, "Too risky . . . only one way in and out. If anyone spotted you the plan would be blown."

To my relief he agreed at once. "You're right," he said. "I'll think on it some."

"I'll be keeping an eye on things and we'll be ready to spring the trap. If the gang doesn't take the bait, or is scared off . . . well, it really will benefit the Bledsoes and we're no worse off than before."

Hume nodded his understanding. "It's your plan, Ryland. And your neck if something does go wrong. How do you want to play it?"

Inwardly I sighed, knowing that as hard as convincing Jim Hume had been, it was still the easiest part of what I had in mind. That thought was not comforting. "Leave it to me," I said. "I'll handle all the theatrical arrangements, and the publicity and so forth. You just play your part. Oh, and give me the names of a couple of absolutely trustworthy men. I won't let them in on the project till the curtain goes up, but I want to know who they are ahead of time."

"Done," he said without hesitation. "Potter and Burson. You can count on them completely and trust them with your life. I'll give them the word to help you out, no matter how . . . odd . . . your request might be. Anything else? I'm going to Richardson's to check on Ollie. Eliza asked me to dinner."

He said that of course to see if it provoked any response from me. Little did he know that Eliza and I had concocted a plan together to keep him as far from the Wells, Fargo office as possible. "No," I said. "Give 'em all my best."

"That I will," he acknowledged, straightening his hat once more. "Be seeing you."

CHAPTER 11

We had already given an afternoon performance for the benefit of the younger audience. At two bits a head we packed them in. We had sold almost two thousand dollars worth of tickets for the night show. Accompanied by Potter and Burson robed as stalking headless figures in black capes carrying jack-o'-lantern heads, I made a great show of placing all the collected proceeds into the company safe. Whether or not the Baker Gang mice came to sniff the Wells, Fargo cheese, it was apparent that the Bledsoes would be well provided for.

I was still wearing my costume: a powdered wig complete with pigtail, knee britches, high stock wrapped up to my chin, and buckle-toed shoes. Tess had applied makeup to hollow my cheekbones and eye sockets, but I regret to say no theatrical device was needed to enhance my Adam's apple. With a little hunching of my back and stooping of my shoulders, I was the very picture of Ichabod Crane.

On the porch outside the Oddfellow's Hall, which was our theater, there was a nice breeze swooping out of the Sierra. My stomach was turning strange somersaults, but not because of stage fright. I studied the town below me, from the jail to distant Chinatown at the far end of Main Street. The lanes were packed with people. The proprietors of Coloma's eateries and bars, quick to take advantage of the carnival atmosphere, opened for business outdoors. The air was full of the smells of roasting pork, sizzling bacon, bubbling cauldrons of beans, and pies of every description.

It was so crowded! How was I to locate anyone acting suspiciously in the midst of such huge numbers of people? How had I ever convinced myself and the sensible Jim Hume that such a scheme would work?

I caught a glimpse of one of the headless horsemen wandering through the throng and gave him a big wave, but he did not respond. Then at the top of the hill east of the river there burst into sight a huge flame, bright orange and illuminating the entire crown of the hill. It had to be a brushfire of immense proportion.

My jaw dropped and I looked around for someone to warn about the conflagration. I was so distracted that Eliza was able to sneak up beside me and tap me on the elbow, making me jump straight up and bump my head on the rafters over the porch. "Startle you?" she asked with a laugh.

Wordlessly I pointed at the gleaming blaze as explanation, then my arm dropped to mimic my jaw as I saw that the flare atop the slope was an enormous harvest moon sailing up into the sky. "Full moon," I mumbled. "Nice touch for the show."

"Yes," Eliza agreed, looking at me closely. "Are you all right?"

"Nervous," I said. "I don't know whether to hope we were right or wrong."

"Oh, Mister Ryland," she corrected. "We must be right. Think of Tom Baker, hiding in fear for his life. How long do you suppose that can go on?"

"You're right," I agreed. Then thinking about our bargain I added, "And, worse luck, he still hasn't stolen anything."

She patted my powdered cheek. "Don't give up hope," she said. "Ling says to tell you that you look a 'plopah Chinnee number one boy.'" When my expression betrayed my lack of comprehension, Eliza reached out and pulled the queue of my wig. "Velly plopah," she mimicked.

I am certain that I blushed under the greasepaint, but do not think she could tell. "I should go get ready for the next performance," I said. At that moment, Tess and Lavinia strolled out and said as much to me. Pushing past Eliza, each of the actresses took one of my elbows. "Come along, sweetie," Tess said, yanking me toward the dressing rooms. "Can't keep your public waiting . . . or us girls, neither."

Now Tess, portraying Ichabod's great love, Katrina van Tassel, was dressed in the costume of the previous century's New Amsterdam Dutch. Nevertheless, the upper half of her torso bore a striking resemblance to the style adopted by saloon girls and the even less respectable females of my own day. Over my shoulder I saw Eliza with a great, dark frown on her face. "'Til later, then, Miss Richardson," I called.

"By all means hurry along," she exclaimed. "Before Miss Darby catches her death of pneumonia."

"What do you suppose she meant by that?" Tess breathed, rubbing against my arm. "I'm not the least bit cold."

We performed the play in three parts. May I say that if the acting by the Hampton Theatrical Company did not enhance Washington Irving's reputation, it did it no harm either. The first act of *The Legend of Sleepy Hollow* was well known. The audience was properly sympathetic to the ungainly schoolmaster and suspicious of Brom Bones. The hulking Bones was played with a melodramatic flair by Frank.

We had been careful to relieve the attendees of their firearms, knives, clubs, and bottles at the door. It was not possible to remove the effects of the hooch they had consumed, so we did get our share of lewd whistles, questionable catcalls, and shouted advice. "Watch out for Bones! He's a bad'un!"

When Katrina was coaxed into sitting alongside me on the piano bench, there were also shouts of, "Watch out for the schoolmaster, darlin'!" And when Katrina and I did a turn on the dance floor, Tyrone, playing Katrina's father, was urged to make his daughter be less of a flirt. I am certain that such careful regard was born more of envy than righteous concern.

Eliza was seated in the front row of the theater, next to Mrs. Bledsoe and the Bledsoe alphabet, who were seeing the show for the second time. Eliza's expression was difficult for me to read beyond the lanterns that served as our footlights. I could not tell if she thought well of the performance or not.

There was an intermission of about fifteen minutes during which the furniture was rearranged to portray the van Tassel living room for Act Two. I was out the back door of the Oddfellow's Hall to confer with one of my headless horsemen. "Nobody has showed the slightest interest in your office," Potter reported. "Me an' Burson been watching turn about. Nothing suspicious a'tall."

I shrugged. "Well, it was a good idea, but not all good ideas pan out. The next act is short. Send Burson up to report and you take a stroll in the alley behind the Metropolitan."

"Why there special?"

"No special reason, just a feeling."

"What am I looking for?"

A string of small explosions chattered on the far side of Coloma, interrupting my reply. It was just as well, since I had nothing concrete to offer. "Who's shooting off the 'crackers?" I asked. "I thought everybody was packed inside the hall."

"Chinese," Potter replied. "Celestials get up a big hooraw for weddings, which they got one of, on accounta the full moon . . . good luck, or something."

"Halloween, headless horsemen, fireworks, but no bandits," I sighed. "Better get back."

Potter turned to go, then stopped. "There is one white fella out and about," he said. "I seen Marshall outside the Metropolitan about an hour ago. Said to tell you that you still owe him for them other pumpkins."

"Sure," I agreed. "If you see him again, tell him I won't forget."

The second act of *Sleepy Hollow* is where Brom Bones gathers the van Tassel family and Ichabod around the fire and tells them the story of the Headless Horseman and the safety that lies beyond the old covered bridge. It is spooky if done well, and Frank was one of the best; pausing to draw out the creepy moments. When he threw a sudden gesture up to the dimly glowing lanterns, the giant shadow of his hand flickered across the audience and made them gasp.

All I had to do was listen attentively and appear to grow more and more nervous; rattling my cup and saucer and that sort of thing. Since I had almost no lines apart from an occasional "Oh, my!" I had plenty of time to think.

If the robbers had not turned up, come tomorrow I would have to face Jim Hume and confess that I had been hiding Baker. I would appeal to Hume to spirit the young man out of town and try to get him a fair trial elsewhere. Of course, I would be finished in Coloma, El Dorado County, and possibly with Wells, Fargo altogether, but what could I do?

Where was Hume anyway? I assumed he had made good on his plan to sneak back to town, but he had sent no word to me.

Then another pair of absences struck me. Where was Judge Magee and where was Tim Flynn? Both were antagonistic toward me enough to stay away for spite, but were they around their usual haunts? I made a mental note to ask Burson if he'd seen them. (Mentally marking that inquiry, I missed a cue and Frank had to repeat his line about "Don't look back!" for me to remember to drop my teacup on the floor. The audience never knew; they thought it was to milk the scariness of the phrase.)

I returned to thinking. Poor old Marshall, drinking away the night. When I paid him for the extra pumpkins, he would probably drink that up, too.

The thought brought me up short. What extra pumpkins? I had paid for seven: three carried by cast members as advertising, the two used as props in the shows, and two more toted by Potter and Burson.

The applause that greeted the end of Act Two interrupted my reverie. We players exited the stage for the canvas scenery to be unrolled and the potted trees to be pushed in that depicted the road through the haunted forest.

Burson had no more interesting news than Potter. No, he had not seen either Flynn or Magee around town. Yes, he would watch for them. He chuckled once during his recital. "Potter must be scared of his own shadow in this getup," he laughed, pinching a handful of black robe as he spoke. "He went down the alley like you said, but he popped out the other end about ten seconds later. He musta run!"

The sound of another string of firecrackers chattering away underscored the ludicrous upshot of the evening.

"The whole night is turning out to be fun and games," I said dryly. "You boys might as well have some merriment, too."

We actually used Ophelia in Act Three. The script called for Ichabod to ride home on the back of an old cob, a broken-down plow horse, as scared of the dark as Crane himself. Talk about casting true to type! Ophelia was an accomplished thespian of course, and even nickered delightedly at being "back in harness" so to speak.

Galloping through dark and tangled forests was not her style, but such athletic effort was not required anyway. All the old mare had to do was amble slowly across the stage while I pretended to whip her furiously and the canvas scenery was unrolled and rolled up again behind her, depicting breakneck speed.

The fiery steed belonging to the evil Headless Horseman was illustrated by means of silhouette shapes displayed on the backdrop, as was the phantom rider himself.

The crashing through the brush, the breathless, heart-stopping ride, the sprint for the bridge . . . all were portrayed in this way, to the rapt attention of the onlookers. All, I say, but the last bit where the apparition rises up in his stirrups, Ichabod makes the mistake of turning to look, and the haunt hurls his head.

At that moment Frank appeared atop a rolling ladder draped in black, making him seem ten feet tall and able to glide over the floor. I turned on cue, he lifted the jack-o'-lantern and flung it, right on target.

All at once, it struck me; both literally and figuratively. I was supposed to ward off the impact of the pumpkin with my forearms, while throwing myself to the ground in simulated catastrophe.

While I succeeded in deflecting the strike of the grinning carved head, I could not escape the sudden realization of what a dupe I had been. Extra pumpkins! Of course! The watchman who had not returned my wave had not been mine! The robbers had seen my play with the costumed guards and raised me one better: they also slipped about town in hooded black robes carrying jack-o'-lanterns.

Tumbling over and over like a bowling ball, I burst out of the side door of the Oddfellow's Hall, just as an explosion rocked the town. Louder than any before, this was no firecracker but the sound of a serious blast; the kind safecrackers used to blow the doors off vaults.

Sliding and sprawling down the hill toward Main Street, I could hear thunderous applause well up behind me. I had no time to feel gratified that my performance had been so well received, although a vagrant thought scooted across my mind that it would be a very surprising curtain call. Just as at the end of the story, Ichabod Crane has disappeared, in our version the actor would really have vanished!

"Burson! Potter!" I yelled. "The office is being robbed. Where are you?"

A cloud of smoke and dust was lifting up from the back of the row of buildings by the river. Glowing eerily pale orange in the gleam of the full moon, it looked like a miniature thundercloud building up over the Wells, Fargo agency.

Another sudden realization: while my guards had been watching the front door and window of my office, the robbers prepared to blast a hole in the rear wall and enter that way. Any second now another explosion would confirm that they had set a charge under the safe.

Out in front of the Sierra Nevada Hotel was a headless horseman figure. "Burson! Potter!" I yelled again. "Get inside quick!"

Instead of acknowledging my shout, the phantom spun on his heel and fled toward the shadows behind the Metropolitan. It had to be one of the robbers! How I wanted to go after him! I desperately needed to catch one of the bandits, but chasing him would mean losing the money in the safe!

As I sprinted toward the office door, out of the alley beside the smithy emerged another headless form. I was right on top of him! "No, you don't!" I barked, vaulting off my buckle-tied shoes and bringing him down in a flying tackle.

We collided with a crash and rolled over together on the boardwalk. He was strong, but I was wiry and I had the upper hand.

"Get off me!" the shadow demanded.

"In a pig's eye!" I retorted. "You're under arrest!"

"It's me, you fool!" my prisoner corrected. "Me! Jim Hume!"

Apologies would have to wait. Yanking the deputy to his feet, we plunged on together toward the express agency. When we were almost there, the door burst open and a man ran out. This one was not dressed as a headless horseman, and neither was a second form close behind. But the pursuer was almost as startling as the headless haunts: a woman, broad of shoulder and thick of waist, darted after the man and slammed into him from behind. I saw the female raise a pair of clenched fists and bring them down hard on the fleeing man's back.

The blow must have had considerable force behind it, because the fugitive's head snapped back, his body staggered forward and he spun around.

"Look out, he's got a gun!" I managed to cry out in warning.

Before the weapon had come up to horizontal, the woman chopped down on the gunman's arm. This blow was followed with a vicious uppercut that rocked the man on his heels. Another blow knocked him clear onto his back. The pistol went flying.

Knees on his chest, the female pugilist pummeled the man's head until he hollered in a rasping voice. "Quit! I give! Quit!"

Jim Hume and I arrived at the same instant. "What is this?" the deputy demanded.

In a decidedly masculine voice the victorious female explained, "This fella blew open the rear wall of the office. 'Bout deafened me, too. When the dust settled he come in and I jumped pert near on top of him. Drew down on me, too, he did, then said, 'Pardon, ma'am,' and he run for the door."

"And who are you?" Hume demanded.

The woman yanked the bonnet from her head. The light coming from the windows of the Metropolitan Hotel revealed the features of Tom Baker!

"Baker!" Hume bellowed, fumbling in the black robe for his pistol. "Then who's this?"

"Easy, Jim," I said. "I can explain. Unless I'm much mistaken the man on the ground is the one who *called* himself Tom Baker; don't know what his real name is, but he's the man who shot Nick Bledsoe."

"Trent, my name is Trent," the captive burst out. "I didn't mean to kill Bledsoe! Get me a fair trial and I'll give you all you need to put the real boss away for keeps."

"Who's that?" Hume demanded.

"Magee," was the reply.

In that night of surprises and weirdly clad apparitions, one would have thought that no stupefactions were left. Yet, when I looked toward the corner of the Metropolitan Hotel, I saw not one, nor two, but three headless horsemen approaching.

"Who's there?" It was my turn to get some of the questioning done.

"Burson and Potter," one of the specters replied. "We caught this fella trying to get to a horse. He woulda made it, too, 'cept his strange getup spooked the critter."

"Pull off his hood," I ordered. "Let's see what we caught."

It was Tim Flynn, of course.

"Where's the rest of the gang?" Hume snarled. "Talk quick before the whole town gets here and I tell them who killed Nick!"

"Don't let 'em lynch me!" Trent begged. "There is no more gang. After Will and the others got kilt, the rest split up. Honest! I only come back because Magee said you was out of the county and that Ryland was a fool!"

"You talk too much!" Flynn snapped. "Keep your yap shut!"

"You ain't the one looking at a noose! It's Magee you want! He planned it all."

"Yes, and killed your partner to keep him from talking," Hume said.

Burson marched the two prisoners off to the lockup, while I posted Potter to guard the shattered office and still-intact safe.

Baker, Hume, and I went in search of Magee. "You don't have to do this," Hume said to Baker by way of apology. "You helped out enough already when you tackled Trent."

"Reckon I'll see it through," Baker allowed. "This Magee fella is the one who put Flynn up to riling the mob to howl for my neck; I kinda owe him a visit."

Finding Magee proved to be tougher than expected. He was nowhere to be found in the Metropolitan Hotel, neither in his office, nor in any of the rooms. "He must have slipped out the back after the explosion," Hume ventured.

"I don't think so," I argued. "Burson and Potter would have seen him. And we know he didn't come out the front. It's almost like he had an escape tunnel."

Hume laughed. "Like you could keep that a secret around here! Why the noise of the digging . . ."

He stopped abruptly and I filled in the rest. "Could have been covered by the crash of the bowling!"

We found the entrance to the shaft behind a thin wall at the end of the third alley. The black passage pointed toward the river. The air was still and thick-feeling. "We're too late," Hume groaned. "He had his horse at the other end and when things went sour, he vamoosed."

"You and Tom go over and locate the outlet," I suggested. "I'll go through the tunnel and meet you."

"All right," Hume agreed. "But we're wasting time. We oughta get up a posse and get after him right now."

"Humor me," I said. "And let me borrow your Colt."

About twenty yards into the shaft, I felt a sudden urge to blow out the lamp I was carrying. I advanced a couple more feet, groping my way along, then crouched on the floor behind a square support timber and felt around for a loose rock. There were many scattered here and there and I grabbed a fist-sized stone and threw it into the blackness ahead of me. As I tossed it, I squeezed my eyes tight shut.

A gunshot exploded. Its muzzle flare illuminated the inside of my eyelids, but did not blind me. The slug sizzled down the wall of the passage. "Magee," I whispered softly, my voice reverberating as if I were out in the listening hills. "Give it up. You're in a bottle and there's no way out."

Another round exploded, and this time I fired back. A cry of pain reached me, then two more gunshots ricochetted off ceiling and walls, nowhere near me.

"Magee," I murmured again. "You are firing blind, and the only way out is past me. It's your call. Do you want to die here?"

I heard the sound of metal clatter to the floor and the judge called out, "Don't shoot! I give up!"

"I wager you've got a lamp or a candle with you," I said. "Light it and walk forward real slow and easy."

That was the way we reentered the basement of the Metropolitan: Magee with his hands in the air, cussing under his breath, and me urging him along with Jim Hume's Colt and a big grin on my face.

Hume met me in the bowling alley and accepted both the return of his weapon and the prisoner. "Found the horse still tied up there. But how'd you know?" he wondered aloud.

"There was no draft of air in the tunnel," I said, "like there should have been if it opened at the river. I just guessed that when Trent blasted the Wells, Fargo office, he collapsed the shaft beneath it. Since Magee could not get out, his only chance was to hope no one would find the tunnel. He was going to hide there till the way was clear to escape."

"The only way clear for him now is straight to the hoosegow," Hume said.

"You've got nothing on me," Magee blustered. "I don't even know what this is all about!"

"Oh, we'll think of something. What do you say, Counselor?"

"Conspiracy for certain," I said in my best lawyer talk, "but I think the State can show that the killing of Downieville Will to hide criminal conspiracy is murder."

EPILOGUE

The gathering at Doc Richardson's house was jovial and excited. Ollie Turnipseed, newly permitted out of bed and stumping around the house on crutches, was particularly jubilant. "Hoo-wee!" he exulted. "Magee and Flynn and the stolen gold. What a night! What a night!"

It was time for congratulations and also explanations. Jim Hume and I were unravelling the tangled skein as best we were able. Tom Baker paid close attention, having the greatest reason to be concerned about the tale. Since being variously locked in jail, belfry, and my attic, he was the one who knew the least. "But why frame me?" he wanted to know.

"Flynn isn't really that bright," Hume answered. "You framed yourself by finding Trent's horse with the bullion. All Flynn did was capitalize on it. It was his thought to get you lynched and take some of the fire out of the town over Nick's death."

"But Magee saw it differently," I continued. "He knew that an escape just before another robbery would cause confusion, which it did. Pedro slipped Ollie some sleeping powder in his coffee. As a judge, Magee already had a key to the jail. Clobbering Ollie on the head and dropping the note from "the Baker Gang" added to the mystery of the escape. And Magee's the one who told Trent to use your name."

"But no one on the Georgetown stage heard the name Tom Baker," Eliza pondered. "Why turn around and use it with Macreedy?"

Jim Hume and I looked at each other and he nodded at me. "Jack figured that one out," he said.

"In the excitement of the holdup, Trent forgot to drop Tom's name," I explained. "He remembered it later when he spotted the light from Macreedy's cabin, just like I did. The whole reason for holding up the old hermit was to use the alias. By the way, we found the poke of gold dust that was taken from the Scotsman in Magee's safe."

I pulled my daddy's watch out and dangled it by the chain. "This is what I cared about getting back," I said.

"That is a right fine timepiece," Tom Baker said, looking at my pocket watch. "Can I see it?"

I passed it over to him. He twirled it and turned it with admiration.

"The gang knew the truth, of course," Hume continued. "Flynn and Magee went along to Michigan Bluff to either help the bandits escape, or, failing that, prevent them from talking."

"Flynn and Trent were both wearing headless horseman getups to spy out the town?" Baker asked.

"Yep," I agreed. "Flynn was supposed to be the lookout at the front of the office while Trent blew a hole in the wall. But you foiled the theft, Tom."

Baker blushed and looked down at his plate of pumpkin pie. Shyly he said, "Guess I need a breath of air." He rose and went out on the porch.

"Has all the stolen property been recovered?" Eliza asked.

Hume shook his head. "Flynn or Magee cached some of the gold from the first holdup, but we'll sweat it out of one of them. Trent and Flynn are both anxious to pin as much as they can on Magee . . . we'll get it all back, never fear."

"So what is left?" I said.

"Marshall," Doc Richardson said. "What about him?"

"Now that Magee won't be around to keep setting up free drinks, maybe he'll dry out," Jim Hume observed.

"Takes more than drying out," Richardson argued. "Man's gotta feel needed . . . and cared about, too. Take me, for example. Now that Eliza is back I'm on the wagon and glad of it."

"How's this for an idea?" I inquired. "Tom there needs a job and James Marshall needs to feel needed. What say Tom works for Marshall and the two of them can watch out for each other?"

"Might work," Richardson agreed. "What do you say, Eliza?"

"I don't know, Dad," she said.

"Eh? Why not?"

"I'm not certain Mister Baker can be trusted."

You could have heard a pumpkin seed hit the floor in the silence that followed her words. "I'm sure it's just a tiny setback," she added. "But, a bargain is a bargain and I'm honor-bound to marry Mister Ryland . . . Tom Baker has just stolen his watch."

HISTORICAL NOTE

In the listening hills of the western Sierra, Coloma, birthplace of the Gold Rush, still exists, but only as a shadow of its former self. The stone jail no longer houses prisoners and the Metropolitan Hotel is long since gone, but Emmanuel Church still stands.

The late 1850s were on the hinge of change for the West. From '49er days, when every mining camp made its own laws at whim, a decade later county and state officials were at least attempting to enforce commonly agreed upon rules of civilization.

Though films make us think that stage robbers were around as long as stages themselves, it was not really so. The first holdup of a coach in the mining region of California only occurred a couple of years prior to the events depicted in this story. In 1857, highway robbery by gangs of bandits was by no means common.

Unfortunately, such criminal activity grew ever more frequent and more sophisticated as time passed. The forces of law and order were also required to become increasingly clever and inventive. Jim Hume became a leading figure in nineteenth-century criminology. He eventually turned his early experiences as a deputy sheriff into a position as chief special officer for Wells, Fargo criminal investigations division.

ABOUT THE AUTHORS

With twenty-four novels to their credit, more than six million books in print, and seven ECPA Gold Medallion awards, Bodie and Brock Thoene have taken their work of historical fiction to the top of the best-seller charts and to the hearts of their readers.

Bodie is the storyteller, weaving plotlines and characters into stunning re-creations of bygone eras.

Brock provides the foundation for Bodie's tales. His meticulous research and attention to historical detail ensure that the books are both informative and entertaining.

The Thoenes' collaboration receives critical acclaim as well as high praise from their appreciative audience.

LOOK FOR THESE OTHER BESTSELLING NOVELS FROM BODIE AND BROCK THOENE

Winds of Promise
A Novel

The first book in the Wayward Wind Series deposits the reader into the life of Rafer Maddox and the gold rush fever that gripped San Francisco in the 1850s. Maddox stumbles into a deadly ring of thievery that threatens all he loves, and brings his soul closer to the will of the Almighty.

0-7852-8072-3 • 224 pages • Trade Paperback

Shiloh Autumn
A Novel

The most heartfelt book the Thoenes have written, this novel is a compelling portrait of an American dust bowl family. Based on Bodie's own grandparents' lives, *Shiloh Autumn* takes readers back to the Great Depression to experience Depression-era life, from possum hunts to mass migration, Penny Auctions to the Veteran's March on Washington. Another Thoene novel destined to become a classic.

0-7852-8066-9 • 480 pages • Hardcover
0-7852-7134-1 • 480 pages • Trade Paperback
0-7852-7273-9 • Audio

Only the River Runs Free
A Novel

A heartrending tale of tyranny and oppression, *Only the River Runs Free* is the first book in the Galway Chronicles. This is a story set in "old country" Ireland in the era that gave birth to the terrorist bombings and class hatred of our time before millions of Irish immigrated to America to escape such persecution. The courage and hope of one family and a child inspire a whole village to challenge and confront those who've abused them. Only the miracle of faith can transform their battered spirits and restore their lives.

0-7852-8067-7 • 304 pages • Hardcover
0-7852-7016-7 • 304 pages • Trade Paperback
0-7852-7128-7 • Audio